CHRISTMAS
STORYBOOK COLLECTION

DISNEY PRESS
New York • Los Angeles

TABLE OF CONTENTS

A Toy Christmas

"Take that!" Andy said in Woody's voice. "You're spending Christmas in jail!" He put Hamm the piggy bank into an old shoebox with slits cut into the sides.

Andy was playing in his room with his toys. In one hand he held Woody the cowboy. In the other was Buzz Lightyear the space ranger.

"You'll be seeing bars for a long, long time," Andy added in Buzz Lightyear's commanding tone.

Andy's mother came into the room and sat down on the bed. "Andy, I have a surprise for you," she said. "You know Christmas is coming up. And this year for your big present . . . we're going to the Grand Canyon!"

Andy dropped Woody and Buzz on the floor. He jumped up and down. "Hooray!" Andy said. "That's the best present ever! Can I take Buzz and Woody?" He picked up his two favorite toys.

"I think it's better if you leave them here," his mother said. "You'll be so busy you won't have any time to play. Now come on. We have a lot to do to get ready."

The moment the door shut behind Andy and his mother, the toys came to life. Buzz sat up. Woody straightened his cowboy hat.

"All right!" Rex the dinosaur said as he came out from under the bed. "The trip is Andy's big present this year. That means no other toys to take our places!"

"I was worried Andy was going to get a video game," Hamm added.

All the toys started talking at once.

"Hold on a minute," Woody said. He walked to the center of the room. "Sure, it's great that there aren't going to be any new toys to replace us. But did you think about what else this means? It means Christmas *without Andy*."

Everyone got quiet. Christmas without Andy? Why, Christmas without Andy wouldn't seem like Christmas at all!

RC's fender drooped sadly. Slinky Dog hung his head. Even the Green Army Men looked glum.

Buzz Lightyear walked over to Woody. "Andy will be gone, but that doesn't mean we can't have Christmas. We'll just make it a toy Christmas!"

Woody looked at the other toys around him. He forced a smile onto his face. "Buzz is right," he said. "We'll have a great Christmas this year."

But deep down, Woody knew it couldn't happen. It was true that they could have their own Christmas. But without the kid who loved them all, it wouldn't be much fun at all.

After Andy and his family left on their trip, the toys started getting ready for Christmas. They had a lot to do. They made decorations, practiced singing songs, and looked for presents for each other.

"Psst, Woody, over here," Jessie hissed loudly. Woody found her hiding behind a stack of books. "Look what I found," she said proudly. She held up a red bandanna.

"Why, Jessie, Bullseye has been looking for his bandanna for months!" Woody said.

"I know." Jessie grinned. "It's going to be a great present for him."

"Come sing some Christmas carols," Wheezy the penguin called to Woody.

"All right," Woody said. He thought maybe the songs would put him in the Christmas spirit.

Wheezy grabbed Mike the tape recorder, and as the music began, his high squeaky voice dropped to a deep baritone. First he belted out a rocking rendition of "Santa Claus Is Coming to Town." Then he glided into a jazzy "Frosty the Snowman." But when Wheezy started crooning "Blue Christmas," Woody had to move away. It made him think of how sad he'd be without Andy.

"Catch you later, Wheezy, Mike," Woody said with a tip of his hat.

Wheezy and Mike continued to sing as Woody walked off. He was glad his friends were in the holiday spirit. But he couldn't stop thinking about how much he missed Andy.

He went over to the other side of the room.

"Hey, Woody, want to help us decorate?" Slinky Dog asked. "Watch this." He gave Woody a poke in the ribs, then yelled, "Hit it!" In a flash, two Aliens bounced superhigh and draped a string of red and green buttons along the edge of the bookcase.

"Pretty neat, Slink," Woody said with an approving nod. "And nice job, Sarge," he called to the army commander and his troops. They were hanging sparkly silver jacks that looked like 3-D snowflakes around the room.

"We've got a Christmas tree, too," Slinky Dog told him. He pointed to a tree made entirely of cotton balls. Red and green hair ribbons were wrapped around it and tied into a bow at the top. There already were presents under the tree. They were wrapped in shiny paper and topped with colorful bows.

"Looks like it's a white Christmas," Sarge said.

Woody smiled a little bit. He was impressed that all the toys were working together to make Christmas a happy holiday.

Woody kept track of the days on the calendar in Andy's room. Finally, it was the big one, December 24th. Christmas Eve.

Hours passed with secrets and whispers, and before long, it grew dark outside. The toys all gathered together to celebrate the holiday, but Woody held back. He was thinking of Andy.

"Hey there, Sheriff," Buzz said. "Why so down? It's a beautiful night out there and . . . it's Christmas Eve!"

"I don't know, Buzz," Woody said. "It's just not the same without Andy."

"You're right," Buzz said. "It's not the same. But you have other friends besides Andy. Come on." He put his arm around Woody's shoulders.

Woody and Buzz walked by Bo Peep. She was reading a Christmas story to the newest toys, the ones who had never had a Christmas before. Bo winked at Woody.

Lo and behold, Woody's heart felt a little lighter.

THE NIGHT BEFORE CHRISTMAS

Then Buzz led Woody over to the Christmas tree. Etch A Sketch stood by the tree, a roaring fire drawn on his screen. Nearby, someone had set up the wooden blocks to spell out "MERRY CHRISTMAS."

"Get the lights, Sarge!" Buzz shouted.

The sarge saluted and turned out the lights.

"Here's a little thing I like to call Christmas magic," Buzz said. He pressed the laser button on his right arm, and a beam of light shot out onto the wall. He pressed the button again and again and again. It was so quick that his finger became a blur. He moved the lights around—to the right, the left, up, down, left, down, right, up. The light pulsed around the dark room, making a show of dancing snowflakes, sugarplums, and lots and lots of toys—dolls, trains, teddy bears.

Woody's jaw dropped and his eyes grew wide. "Wow, Buzz," the cowboy said. "That's really great! I didn't know you could—"

His sentence was cut off by a jolly "Ho, ho, *rrrrroar*!" as RC rolled into the circle. RC was decorated to look like a sleigh. And following behind him was Rex with a white cotton beard and a red sock hat.

"Sorry about the roar," Rex said, even though no one had been scared. "Sometimes I forget I'm Santa Claus, not a fierce bone-crunching carnivorous dinosaur!"

Rex went to the Christmas tree. He picked up presents to give to each and every toy. Bullseye was thrilled to have his bandanna back. Mr. Spell got brand-new batteries.

"Your speaking was getting a little slow there," Slinky Dog pointed out.

Buzz got a Star Command four-way outer space signal interceptor. His friends had put it together out of a small cardboard box, some sequins from an old doll dress, and lots of duct tape.

"Thanks, guys!" he said. "It's just what I always wanted!"

One of the dolls gave Jessie a dress. Hamm's present was a quarter.

"Woo-hoo," he shouted. "That's as good as twenty-five pennies! Five nickels! Two dimes and a nickel! I'm feeling flush!"

And then Bo Peep pulled Woody over and gave him a big kiss. He turned as red as the Christmas lights. "Aw shucks, Bo," he said.

Woody looked at his friends. Buzz was right. Christmas without Andy wasn't better or worse. It was different. Spending time with people—and toys—you loved was what Christmas was really all about.

"Hey, Buzz, Woody, everyone!" Slinky Dog yelled from the edge of the bed. "Check this out!" He pulled the window curtain aside. Outside, snow drifted down.

"It's a white Christmas!" he shouted. "Merry Christmas, everyone!"

Woody smiled. "Merry Christmas," he replied.

Ghosts of Christmas Past

It should have been a joyous time. Christmas was coming—
Rapunzel's very first Christmas since returning home to the castle.
She had spent every Christmas locked away in Mother Gothel's
tower since she was a baby.

The castle halls were decked with boughs of holly. The butlers
had just chosen the royal Christmas tree. Everyone did their best to
spread holiday cheer. Even the crankiest townsfolk were merry.

But in the royal family, one person was *not* ready for a happy holiday. "No way. Uh-uh," said Rapunzel. "I refuse to celebrate Christmas!"

"What?" cried Flynn. "Why don't you want to celebrate the most wonderful holiday of the year?"

Rapunzel looked shocked. "Wonderful?" she said. "I think you mean 'terrifying'!"

Flynn was confused—until Rapunzel shared her memories of Christmases spent in Mother Gothel's tower.

"You know how it is," Rapunzel said. "There's all of that eerie Christmas music. Mother Gothel sang it nonstop at Christmastime. I hate chanting and growling."

That didn't sound like any Christmas music Flynn had ever heard. But he let Rapunzel continue: "Mother Gothel also told us the tale of Nicholas, the ghostly Christmas elf—how he creeps into children's rooms on Christmas Eve and steals them away. It kept me up at bedtime!" Rapunzel sighed and shrugged. "But I guess that's why all kids have trouble sleeping on Christmas Eve."

"Actually, no!" Flynn said. "That's not what Christmas is like at all!" It was clear to Flynn: Mother Gothel had made Christmas sound frightening on purpose. It was just another way she had tried to make Rapunzel afraid of the world outside her tower.

He smiled, taking Rapunzel by the hand. "You know what?" he said. "I'll show you what Christmas is really like. Come on!"

Flynn took Rapunzel outside the castle. She seemed unsure and a little skittish, but Flynn reassured her. "Just look around—and listen," he said. "Does this seem like a spooky holiday to you?"

They passed a group of children singing Christmas carols. The sound was sweet and soothing. The words were all about hope and joy. It was like no Christmas music Rapunzel had ever heard before.

Just then, a small boy ran up to Rapunzel. He held out a package wrapped with a bow. "Merry Christmas, Princess Rapunzel!" he said. "I made this for you!"

But Rapunzel didn't take the gift. Her eyes widened in alarm. "Trick package! Duck!" she cried, diving for cover behind a low stone wall.

She peeked out warily from her hiding place. Flynn and the children stared at her in disbelief.

"It's not a trick," Flynn said. "Just a gift." He opened the box. Inside was a handwoven crown of evergreens.

Slowly, Rapunzel walked over to him and took the crown. She placed it on her head. "A real Christmas gift?" she said as if she hadn't heard of such a thing. "Not an exploding trick package?" She knelt by the little boy and took his hands in hers. "Thank you so much!"

Next Flynn and Rapunzel came across a tree-trimming party. Together, the townsfolk were decorating an enormous Christmas tree in the center of the town square.

Rapunzel pointed toward the top of the tree. "You need a lot more charms up there," she advised, "if you want to scare off the ghostly Christmas elf." She picked up one of the ornaments. "And I'm not sure these charms are anywhere near scary enough."

Flynn took her aside. "They're not charms," he explained. "They're ornaments. For decoration."

Rapunzel looked confused. "Oh. Well, then, how do you keep the Christmas elf away?"

Flynn couldn't help laughing. "Okay, next lesson . . ."

They went back
inside the castle,
where Flynn read
to Rapunzel from
several books about
St. Nicholas.

"Oh! We had
this one at the
orphanage," Flynn
said, holding up a
red-and-green book.
"See, St. Nicholas
isn't a ghostly
Christmas elf. He's a
jolly old fellow who travels far and wide on Christmas Eve, bringing
gifts to all the boys and girls."

Flynn showed Rapunzel drawings of a smiling bearded man carrying a sack full of presents. "Definitely no kidnapping."

Rapunzel and Pascal looked at each other, marveling at the idea. And to think of all those Christmas Eves they'd spent huddled together by the fire, too afraid to sleep! "You mean, children have trouble sleeping on Christmas Eve because they are excited?" she asked.

Flynn nodded. "That's right," he said. "So, now that you know what Christmas is really like, do you think you might be interested in celebrating it this year? For real? For the first time?"

Rapunzel's face lit up. "Yes!" she replied, and she sprang into action.

For weeks, Rapunzel lived and breathed Christmas, enjoying everything that the holiday season had to offer—everything she had missed out on while living in the tower.

In the castle kitchen, she helped bake dozens and dozens of Christmas cookies.

She learned every word of every Christmas carol she had never heard before.

She decked every undecked inch of hall with garlands and ribbon, and for the first time, she made beautiful—not spooky—Christmas ornaments.

Finally, she wrapped handmade gifts for each member of her family. She could hardly wait until Christmas to see them opened.

By the time Christmas Eve arrived, Rapunzel was exhausted, but very, very happy. Her family gathered to celebrate around their Christmas tree.

Rapunzel's father, the King, proposed a toast. "For years, our hearts have not felt whole at this time of year, because an important part of them was missing." He smiled at Rapunzel.

The Queen raised her glass and added, "But now, for the first time since you were born, Rapunzel, this holiday is a joyful one—for all of us."

Rapunzel couldn't agree more. Surrounded by her warm, loving family, in front of the crackling fire, she could not imagine a better Christmas.

Rapunzel sighed happily and flopped down next to Flynn on a cozy settee. "Thank you. For all of this," she said.

"I should really be thanking you," Flynn admitted. "You know, this is my first Christmas with a real family. All those years in the orphanage, I knew what Christmas was supposed to be like, but it somehow never felt that merry. Until now."

Flynn and Rapunzel sat together in front of the fire, waiting for Christmas to come. But before long, Rapunzel fell asleep.

Flynn smiled. After all those spooky, sleepless Christmas Eves in the tower, Rapunzel had certainly earned a peaceful holiday. It had been a wonderful Christmas Eve. And there would be many more like it for years to come.

Disney
MICKEY MOUSE

Mickey's Christmas Carol

It was snowing in London, England, on Christmas Eve. Ebenezer Scrooge, the richest man in town, hurried toward his office.

"Merry Christmas!" someone shouted.

"Bah, humbug," Scrooge muttered. He didn't know why everyone had to be so cheerful at Christmastime.

When Scrooge reached the door to his office, he looked up at the sign. It read SCROOGE & MARLEY. But Marley's name was crossed out. He'd been dead for seven years.

Scrooge and Jacob Marley had tricked people who didn't have much into giving them money. They had gotten very rich and hadn't cared that they'd been unfair.

Scrooge cackled as he thought of all his money.

38

Bob Cratchit, Scrooge's clerk, was just about to throw a piece of coal into the stove when Scrooge walked in.

"What are you doing?" Scrooge growled.

"I was just trying to thaw out the ink," Bob replied. He gave his boss a small but hopeful smile.

Scrooge knocked the coal out of Bob's hand and scowled. "You used a piece last week! Get back to work," he said.

Bob quickly turned back to his desk.

After a few moments, Bob snuck a glance at his boss. Then he said, "Speaking of work, Mr. Scrooge . . . tomorrow is Christmas. And I was just wondering if . . . if I might have the day off?"

Scrooge was silent for a long time. "Very well," he finally said. "But make sure you come in early the day after!"

Scrooge hung up his jacket and hat. Then he sat down at his desk and began to count his money. "Heh, heh, heh . . . money, money, money!" he crowed.

Suddenly, the door burst open. A young duck carrying a wreath walked in.

"Merry Christmas!" the man said. It was Scrooge's nephew Fred.

"Christmas?" Scrooge scoffed. "Bah, humbug!"

Fred walked up to Scrooge's desk and gave him the wreath. He thought the office could use some holiday cheer.

"Uncle, I've come to invite you to Christmas dinner tomorrow," Fred said with a smile.

"Oh?" Scrooge asked as he came out from behind his desk. "And will there be plum pudding and sugar cakes and a plump roast goose?"

"Oh, yes!" Fred replied. He nodded his head and smacked his lips.

"You know I can't eat that stuff! Now get out!" Scrooge got up and opened the door. He hung the wreath over Fred's neck and pushed his nephew out into the cold.

As Scrooge walked back to his desk, the door opened again.

Fred smiled and hung the wreath on the inside doorknob. Then he closed the door.

Later that night, as Scrooge walked home, he had a strange feeling that he was being followed.

When he reached his front door, he looked at the knocker. It was a lion's head. But as Scrooge stared at it, it began to change before his eyes. Suddenly, Scrooge was looking at the face of his old partner, Jacob Marley! "Ahh!" Scrooge yelled.

Scrooge hurried inside and up to his bedroom. He closed the door and climbed into his chair. He heard the sounds of clanking chains. He shivered, too afraid to move.

Then a ghost appeared beside him! It was Jacob Marley. He was covered in heavy chains.

"Ebeneeezer," the ghost wailed. He rattled his chains. "Do you know who I am?"

Scrooge peered at the ghost from under his top hat.

"When I was alive, I robbed from widows and took money from the poor," Jacob said.

"You were a fine partner, Jacob," Scrooge said with a smile.

"No!" Jacob replied. "I was wrong. And now I have to carry these chains forever as punishment. The same thing will happen to you. Tonight, you will be visited by three spirits. If you don't listen to them, your chains will be heavier than mine."

Then Jacob's ghost disappeared.

Scrooge was still shaking with fear as he got ready for bed. After checking his room for more ghosts, he climbed under the covers. "Humbug," he muttered. Then he fell asleep.

But it wasn't long before a noise woke him up. *Ding! Ding! Ding!* His clock bell was ringing. Scrooge opened his eyes to find a little cricket in a top hat on his bedside table.

"I am the Ghost of Christmas Past," the cricket said. "We're going to visit your past tonight."

The ghost went to the window and pushed it open.

"Just hold on," the ghost said as he hopped into Scrooge's hand.

Scrooge did as the cricket said, and they flew out into the darkness.

The city passed slowly beneath them as they flew high above snow-covered rooftops.

The first stop Scrooge and the Ghost of Christmas Past made was at a little shop. A party was taking place inside.

Scrooge looked through the window.

"It's old Fezziwig's!" he exclaimed. He saw his old boss and many of his dearest friends laughing and dancing inside.

Then he saw Isabelle, the girl he had once loved. She was dancing with a young duck. It was Scrooge—back before he had become old and greedy.

As if reading Scrooge's mind, the ghost said, "In ten years' time, you learned to love something else much more."

The spirit showed Scrooge another scene. Isabelle and Scrooge were in his counting house.

"Ebenezer," Isabelle said softly, "have you made a decision about getting married?"

"I have," Scrooge replied. "The last payment on your cottage was late." Then he told her he was taking the cottage away.

Isabelle began to cry.

As Scrooge watched, he shook his head.

"Remember, Scrooge," the ghost said. "You made these memories."

Scrooge found himself back in his bed again. Then he heard a loud voice say, "I am the Ghost of Christmas Present."

Scrooge looked up and saw a giant. The giant lifted him up and carried him out into the night. He brought Scrooge to a shabby little house. Through the window, Scrooge saw Bob Cratchit with his family. They were having Christmas dinner.

On the table sat the smallest bird Scrooge had ever seen. "Surely they have more food than that," he whispered.

Then a smaller boy hobbled into the room on a crutch. His name was Tiny Tim.

Tiny Tim looked at the meal on the table. "We must thank Mr. Scrooge!" he exclaimed.

Scrooge turned around to ask about Tiny Tim, but the ghost was gone. He was all alone in a graveyard. Suddenly, he saw a dark figure.

"Are you the Ghost of Christmas Future?" Scrooge asked.

The ghost was silent. He pointed to a gravestone.

Scrooge saw the Cratchit family without Tiny Tim. They were near his grave, crying.

The spirit pointed to an empty pit.

"Whose lonely grave is this?" Scrooge asked. Then he realized it was his.

"I can change!" Scrooge cried. "Let me change!"

Suddenly, Scrooge was in his bed again. He ran to the window and looked outside. The sun was shining. The streets were covered with snow. Christmas bells were ringing.

"It's Christmas morning!" he cried. "The spirits have given me another chance!"

He pulled on his hat and coat and ran outside. "Merry Christmas!" he called to everyone he passed.

He saw his nephew, Fred, on the street. "I'm looking forward to that wonderful meal of yours!" he called as he ran by.

Bob Cratchit heard a loud knock on his front door. He opened it to find Mr. Scrooge on the step, holding a large bag.

Scrooge dumped the sack on the floor. Dozens of toys fell out. Scrooge smiled as the children rushed forward happily.

"Bob Cratchit," Scrooge said, "I'm giving you a raise and making you my partner!"

Then he handed a large turkey to Mrs. Cratchit.

"Merry Christmas!" he said happily.

"Merry Christmas to us all," said Tiny Tim.

DUMBO

Dumbo's First Christmas

One December morning, Dumbo the flying elephant woke up to find the circus grounds strangely quiet. He stuck his head outside his tent. Where was everyone?

Then Timothy Mouse appeared. "It's Christmas vacation," he announced. "Time to sleep late, play in the snow, and get ready for the holidays!"

Dumbo looked puzzled.

"Aw, don't tell me you've never heard of Christmas before," Timothy said in disbelief.

"Hey, fellas," he called up to the crows, "come on down here. I need help explaining Christmas to Dumbo."

The birds gathered around the elephant and began to chatter all at once.

"Why, Christmas is packages wrapped up in shiny paper."

"Now wait a minute! What about fancy holiday food?"

"Don't forget a big tree covered in ornaments and lights."

"And music! You can't have Christmas without carols!"

"Now do you understand?" Timothy asked Dumbo.

The elephant shook his head. He was even more confused.

"Hmmm," Timothy said, "this is gonna be harder than I thought." He and the crows huddled together and quickly came up with a new plan.

"Dumbo," said Timothy, "forget telling you about Christmas, we're gonna *show* you!"

Timothy Mouse scampered up onto Dumbo's cap. "Get ready for takeoff!" he cried.

The crows took to the sky. Dumbo flapped his ears and followed right behind them. They flew and flew until, finally, a magnificent skyline came into view.

"Welcome to New York City!" Timothy announced. "I can't think of a more Christmasy place—except maybe the North Pole!" Timothy had grown up in New York and thought it was the best place on Earth.

The little mouse gave Dumbo a tour of the bustling city. He showed the elephant the most festive place in New York first.

"That's Rockefeller Center," Timothy pointed out as they flew over a large tree.

Below, ice skaters glided and twirled around a sparkling outdoor rink. But Dumbo couldn't take his eyes off the enormous tree, covered from top to bottom in twinkling lights and pretty decorations.

Timothy could tell that Dumbo was impressed. "What did I tell you?" the mouse asked. "People here don't just deck the halls—they decorate *everything*!"

Dumbo looked at all the people on the streets, full of holiday cheer. Some carried brightly wrapped packages. Some were singing carols. Everyone was in awe of the great big tree.

The sights and sounds of Christmas made Dumbo feel very happy. He couldn't wait to find out more about the holiday!

Timothy Mouse and Dumbo flew down Fifth Avenue, where the shop windows were filled with beautiful Christmas displays. Dumbo watched the shoppers hurrying around with large bags of presents.

But Timothy saw something else. "Hmm, that's strange," he said. "People keep leaving presents in a box in front of that store over there. Come on, let's go find out what's going on."

When Dumbo swooped down closer to the crowd, everyone cheered. They had never seen a flying elephant before. Dumbo felt like he was performing in one of his shows.

"What are the presents for?" Timothy Mouse asked a woman. "Is it the store's birthday or something?"

The woman chuckled. Then she explained that the packages were toys for children. "There's just one problem," she continued. "The snow has slowed down traffic, and I don't know how we're going to make all our deliveries in time. The boys and girls will be so disappointed if they don't get their presents this year!"

Timothy looked at Dumbo. Dumbo looked at Timothy. "Are you thinking what I'm thinking?" the mouse asked.

Dumbo nodded enthusiastically.

"Lady," said Timothy, "Dumbo and I would be happy to help spread a little Christmas cheer. I know this city like the back of my hand, and Dumbo here never needs to worry about stuff like traffic. You can consider those presents as good as delivered!"

The people on the sidewalk cheered. "Thank you, Dumbo," one man said. "I knew Santa had flying reindeer, but I didn't know he had a flying elephant!"

"Shhh," Timothy replied with a mischievous wink. "It's supposed to be a secret!"

Soon Dumbo was given a sack of presents and a long list of names and addresses.

"Ho, ho, ho!" Timothy called out as he and Dumbo flew off.

The pair arrived at their first stop. Through the window, they could see children hanging stockings over the fireplace. When they saw Dumbo and Timothy Mouse they shouted with joy. Timothy handed each child a brightly wrapped present.

"Thank you!" the children cried as Dumbo and Timothy flew away. "And Merry Christmas!"

Dumbo and Timothy flew from one house to another. They dropped off dolls and dump trucks, books and building blocks, puppets and puzzles. Every once in a while, the crows took a break from sightseeing to pitch in and sing some Christmas music. They were the funniest carolers the kids had ever seen!

Timothy's favorite part was watching the children and their parents when they spied Dumbo outside their windows. They'd blink and rub their eyes, wondering if what they were seeing could possibly be real.

"What's the matter?" Timothy would say playfully. "Haven't you ever seen a flying elephant before?" Then he'd laugh.

But what Dumbo loved most was the way the children's faces lit up when he gave them their presents. It made him feel happy right down to his toes.

"We'll come back to visit them again soon, Dumbo," said Timothy as they headed for home. "I promise."

Back at the circus grounds, Timothy and Dumbo settled down for the night. "So, Dumbo," Timothy asked, "*now* do you know what Christmas is all about?"

Dumbo wasn't listening, though. He was thinking of all the children he had met that day, and how he and Timothy had made them all smile. It had been a perfect first Christmas.

Seeing Dumbo's happy expression, Timothy said, "Yup, I think you do."

The two tired friends soon fell fast asleep. That night, for the first time ever, Dumbo's dreams—and his heart—were filled with the magic of Christmas.

The Sweetest Christmas

One snowy Christmas
Eve, Winnie the Pooh
looked up and down, in
and out, and all around
his house.

He had a tree set up
in his living room. It
was decorated with some
candles in honey pots.

Pooh looked at the
tree and tapped his head.
"Something seems to be
missing," he said.

He walked over to the
window and peered outside. Then he walked back to the tree and
thought some more.

Suddenly, a knocking sound startled Pooh. *Rap-a-tap-tap!* He turned toward his front door.

"Maybe whatever it is I can't remember I'm missing is outside my door," Pooh said.

When Pooh opened the door, he found a small snowman on his front step.

"H-h-he-l-l-l-o, P-Pooh B-Bear," the snowman said as he shivered.

Pooh thought the voice sounded very familiar. He invited the snowman inside.

After standing beside the fire for a few minutes, the snowman began to melt. The more he melted, the more he started to look like Piglet!

"Oh, my," said Pooh. He was happy to see his friend where there used to be a snowman.

"Oh, my," said Piglet. Now that the snow had melted off him, he could see Pooh's glowing Christmas tree.

"Are you going to string popcorn for your tree?" Piglet asked.

"There was popcorn and string," Pooh admitted. "But now there is only string."

Pooh thought some more, wondering if popcorn was what he'd forgotten. But that wasn't it, either.

"Then we can use the string to wrap the presents you're giving," Piglet said.

Something began to tickle at Pooh's brain. It was the something missing that he hadn't been able to remember.

"I forgot to get presents!" Pooh exclaimed.

"Don't worry, Pooh," Piglet said. "I'm sure you'll think of something."

Soon it was time for Piglet to go home and wrap his own presents. He said good-bye to his friend and went back out into the cold, snowy night.

Pooh stood beside his tree and tapped his head while he thought. Where could he find presents for his friends? It was already Christmas Eve. Was it too late?

He thought some more. He sat down in his cozy chair. Then he got up and had a small snack of honey. He peered out the window and watched the snow fall.

Then he had an idea.

He still didn't know what to do about the presents he'd forgotten. But he knew where to find help.

"Hello!" Pooh called as he knocked on Christopher Robin's door.

Christopher Robin opened the door and smiled when he saw the visitor. "Come in, Pooh Bear," he said. "Merry Christmas! Why do you look so sad on the most wonderful night of the year?"

Pooh was just about to explain about the forgotten presents when something caught his eye. He pointed at the stockings over the fireplace. "What are those for?" he asked.

"Those are stockings to hold Christmas presents," explained Christopher Robin.

"But Christopher Robin," Pooh said, "what if someone forgot to find presents for his friends? And what if that same someone doesn't have stockings to hang because he doesn't wear any?"

Pooh looked down at his bare feet, then back up at Christopher Robin.

"Silly old bear," Christopher Robin said. He took Pooh up to his room. They dug through his drawers until Pooh found seven stockings.

"Thank you, Christopher Robin," Pooh said. He smiled. He'd picked a stocking for each of his friends to put their presents in: purple for Piglet, red-and-white striped for Tigger, orange for Rabbit, yellow for Eeyore, maroon for Gopher, and blue for Owl. And one for him to hang over his fireplace.

He hurried off to deliver the stockings to his friends. As he walked through the Hundred-Acre Wood, he thought about the presents he still needed for the stockings.

"I will get the presents later," Pooh said to himself. "The stockings come first."

Pooh stopped at each of his friends' houses. Everyone was asleep. He quietly hung the stockings where his friends would find them. Each one had a tag that read: FROM POOH.

When Pooh got back to his house, he climbed into his cozy chair in front of a roaring fire.

"Now I must think about presents for my friends," he said.

But Pooh was tired from finding the stockings and delivering them to his friends' houses. Before he knew it, his thinking turned into dreaming. He was fast asleep.

The next morning, Pooh awoke to a loud thumping noise. *Thump-a-bump-bump!*

"I wonder who that could be," he said. He climbed out of his chair and opened the door.

"Merry Christmas, Pooh!" his friends cried.

There on Pooh's doorstep stood Tigger, Rabbit, Piglet, Owl, Eeyore, and Gopher. They were each carrying a stocking from Pooh.

Pooh scratched his head. All of a sudden he remembered what had happened the night before. He had fallen asleep before giving presents to his friends!

"Oh, bother," he said. Then he realized that his friends were all talking at once. They were thanking him for their gifts!

"No more cold ears in the winter with my new cap," Piglet said.

"My stripedy sleeping bag is tiggerific!" exclaimed Tigger.

"So is my new carrot cover," Rabbit said.

"This rock-collecting bag will sure make work go faster," Gopher said.

Eeyore swished his tail to show Pooh his new tail-warmer. "No one's ever given me such a useful gift before," he said.

Owl told Pooh his new wind sock would help him with the day's weather report.

Pooh looked at his friends. They were very happy with their stockings, even though there weren't any presents in them!

"Something very nice is going on," Pooh said.

"It is very nice, Pooh Bear," Piglet said.

"It's called Christmas, buddy bear," Tigger said. He patted Pooh on the back.

Then Pooh watched in surprise as each of his friends put a honey pot in Pooh's own stocking.

"I don't know what to say," Pooh told his friends. He was thrilled by their gifts. Honey was his favorite treat!

"Christmas is a wonderful holiday," Rabbit said. "Especially when you have good friends to share it with."

"Yep!" Tigger agreed. "But I know how we could make the day even sweeter."

He looked at the honey pot in Pooh's hands.

An idea tickled at Pooh's brain. "Let's all have lunch together," Pooh said. He passed out the honey pots his friends had just brought him. "Christmas . . . what a sweet day, indeed."

Disney Bambi

The Wonderful Winter Tree

Bambi awoke one morning to find the whole world covered in a soft white blanket.

"What is it, Mother?" Bambi asked as he gazed around in wonder.

"This is snow," replied his mother. "It means winter is upon us."

"Snow!" said Bambi. He took a cautious step . . . and then

another . . . and another. He felt the icy crystals crunch under his hooves. He looked back at the tiny tracks he had made. "I *like* snow!" Bambi said.

"Snow is pretty to look at," his mother told him, "but it makes winter hard for all the animals."

Bambi was about to ask her why winter was harder than other seasons. But just then, his friend Thumper came hopping over.

"Hiya, Bambi!" said the bunny. "Come on! Let's go sliding!" He led Bambi to the pond, which was frozen solid.

Thumper slapped at the ice with his foot. "Come on! It's all right," he told Bambi. "See? The water's stiff!"

Bambi saw his friend, Flower the skunk.

"You want to come sliding?" Bambi called, running over. "Thumper says the water's stiff."

But Flower shook his head. "No, thanks. I'm off to my den. I'm going to sleep through the winter." He yawned. "Good-bye, Bambi," he said.

"'Bye, Flower," said Bambi. Then he spied another friend, a squirrel, scurrying up an oak tree.

"The pond is stiff, Squirrel," called Bambi. "Want to come sliding with me?"

"Thanks," replied the squirrel as he ducked into a hollow in the tree, "but I have to store nuts for the long winter." He showed Bambi the pile he had already collected. "No sliding for me today."

So Bambi headed back to Thumper and the ice-covered pond by himself.

By that time, Thumper was sliding across the ice with some of his sisters. They made it look so easy. But when Bambi stepped on the ice, he lost his balance right away. His hooves went sliding in four different directions!

"Kind of wobbly, aren't ya," said Thumper. He laughed. "Come on, Bambi. You can do it!"

But Bambi wasn't so sure. Sliding across the stiff water wasn't quite as much fun for deer, it seemed, as it was for rabbits. And it also made him hungry. He said good-bye to the bunnies and went back to find his mother.

"Mother, I'm hungry," Bambi told her.

In the spring, summer, and fall, they had been able to find food almost anywhere they looked. But now that it was winter, Bambi could see that finding food wasn't so easy. There were no leaves on the trees, and the grass was covered with snow and ice. The snow was so cold that when he poked through it, Bambi thought his nose might freeze.

At last Bambi's mother uncovered a small patch of grass. Bambi nibbled it eagerly.

Then Bambi curled up with his mother for a nap. The ground was hard and cold and the wind was chilly. Bambi was grateful to have his mother there to keep him warm.

"Is this why the birds fly south and why our other friends sleep through the winter?" Bambi asked her.

His mother nodded and snuggled even closer. "But don't worry, Bambi," she told him. "Winter doesn't last forever."

By the end of December, it seemed
like there was nothing left in the
forest but bitter bark for Bambi
to eat. The days grew short
and the nights grew long,
and throughout them Bambi's
stomach rumbled. And then
one day, something truly
amazing happened.

Thumper was the first
to see it. "Hey, Bambi!" he
hollered. "Would you look at
that tree!"

Bambi followed Thumper's
paw. He could not believe
his eyes.

There before them was a tall pine tree unlike any Bambi had
ever seen. It was draped with strings of bright berries and yummy
popcorn, and from the end of each
branch hung a ripe, juicy apple.
But the most wonderful thing
to Bambi was the gold star
at the very top.

"Mother!" exclaimed
Bambi. "Look what
Thumper found!"
Cautiously, his
mother drew closer.
"It can't be . . ." she
whispered. "It seems
almost too good to be
true."

"What *is* it, Mother?" Bambi asked her.

"The most beautiful tree in the world," she answered. She smiled down at Bambi. "What a special gift to have on your first Christmas."

"Who left it, Mother?" Bambi asked.

"I don't know," she replied.

"Maybe someone who loves animals," Thumper said, hopping up and down. "This is the best gift ever." He sniffed one of the apples hanging low to the ground.

"Can we share this food with every one of our friends, Mother?" Bambi asked.

"Yeah, and with my sisters, too?" Thumper chimed in.

"I don't see why not," Bambi's mother said. "Christmas is a time to share what we have with those we love."

Bambi and Thumper danced happily around the tree. "Look at all the popcorn and berries!" Thumper cried. "And look at that star at the tippy-top, too!"

Bambi stopped prancing. He looked up at the golden star at the top of the tree. Then he looked up at the sky above him. The sun was just beginning to go down. He knew that very soon, there would be a star twinkling in the sky just like the one at the top of the tree. A gentle hush fell over the clearing.

He danced back over to his mother and took a big bite out of one of the juicy green apples. *Mmm!* he thought. Nothing had ever tasted so good!

Gazing up at the star and at the wonderful winter tree, Bambi could feel a happy, warm glow swelling inside him. There was enough food on the tree to feed all the animals who were hungry. What a magical gift, thought Bambi. Winter *was* long and hard . . . and yet wonderful, after all.

The Best Present Ever

"Hey, Lightning—look at me! *Woooo-eeeee!*"

Mater sledded past his best buddy, Lightning McQueen. It was wintertime in Radiator Springs. Christmas was just a few days away, and fresh snow blanketed the ground. The two friends were taking turns sliding down a snow-covered hill using Mater's one-of-a-kind junkyard sled.

"I'm tellin' you, this here's the best sled in Radiator Springs!" Mater exclaimed.

"I know, you *have* told me." Lightning laughed. "Several times. It has its own headlights, superfast gliders—"

"And built-in bumper tires!" the friends said together.

"Well, hold your horsepower," said Mater. "Because it's gonna be even funner when we take it sledding at Kersploosh Mountain!"

Kersploosh Mountain was a water park near Radiator Springs. For just one day a year, on Christmas, the waterslides were frozen over so that cars could go sledding down the chutes.

"Uh, Mater, there's something I need to tell you." Lightning looked worried. "Remember that Russian Ice Racers Cup I told you I'm competing in?"

"Well, sure," said Mater. "The one in a few weeks."

"That's just it," Lightning said. "They moved it up to this week. I'm not going to be here for Christmas after all."

Mater stopped dead in his tracks. "You're not?"

Lightning shook his head. "I'm really sorry, buddy. I know I'll miss Christmas at Kersploosh Mountain. But hey, maybe we can do something else when I get back?"

"Yeah . . . sure thing," Mater said.

Later that afternoon, Mater pulled into Flo's V8 Café.

"Hey there, Mater," Flo called. "Want to try a sip of my new eggnog oil? It's guaranteed to fill you up with Christmas cheer."

"I could use some," said Mater. "I'm plumb out of Christmas cheer."

"Something got you down, honey?" Flo asked.

Mater sighed. "Lightning won't be home for Christmas. He's in some Rushin' Rice Cup."

"That's too bad," Flo said. "I guess you'll have to celebrate the holiday early."

"Yeah, celebrate early! That's a good idea!" said Mater. Then he thought for a moment. "Oh, shoot, I forgot about presents. I've gotta get Lightning something! But what?"

Flo looked thoughtful. "Hmmm. Well, you're going to miss him while he's away, right?"

"Yeah." Mater nodded eagerly.

"So how about getting him something for the race, so he knows you'll be thinking of him? Like ear-mufflers? Or a snow scraper?"

Mater smiled. "Or snow tires! That's a great idea, Flo. I know just where to go!" With that, Mater dashed off.

"Luigi!" Mater yelled as he skidded up to Casa Della Tires. "I need your help!"

Luigi smiled. "For you, Mater, anything!"

"Those snow tires," said Mater. "The ones that used to be in your front window. Where'd they go? I need to buy them for Lightning for his Crushin' Dice Cup!"

Luigi's smile faded. "Ah . . . I can do anything but that. I'm afraid someone's already bought them. They just left a moment ago."

Sure enough, outside, a big truck was driving away from the shop.

Mater raced after the truck, finally catching up with him at the intersection. Mater explained the situation, then pleaded with the truck. "I need those tires for my best buddy's Christmas gift. I'll give you anything."

The truck sighed. "Sorry, but I've been dreaming of speeding through the snow with these superfast tires."

Mater raised an eyebrow. "Fast, huh? What if I told you I had something that goes even faster than those tires?"

Curious, the truck agreed to meet Mater at the edge of town. Meanwhile, Mater raced to his junkyard to grab his sled.

"All right," Mater said when the two trucks met again. "I'll bet my sled is faster going down that hill than you in those tires. If I'm right, we'll trade. Deal?"

The truck agreed, and soon they were zipping down the snowy slope. Mater zoomed past the truck—and won!

The truck happily traded the tires for Mater's sled.

Meanwhile, Lightning was helping Sally decorate the Cozy Cone Motel.

"I feel awful," he said. "Mater looked so sad when I told him."

"Well," said Sally. "Do you *need* to do the race?"

"Huh?" asked Lightning.

"It's not part of your normal circuit," Sally pointed out. "I'm sure they'd understand if you didn't go."

Lightning's eyes lit up. "You're right. Mater is my best friend. And a trophy is just another trophy. I'm going to withdraw from the race and stay here for Christmas!"

Lightning raced home to call Vitaly Petrov, who was hosting the Ice Racers Cup. Vitaly told Lightning not to worry—he could reschedule the race for after the holiday.

"That works out great. Thanks, Vitaly!" said Lightning.

He couldn't wait to tell Mater the good news. On his way to see his best buddy, Lightning drove past a big sign for Kersploosh Mountain. He suddenly had an idea for the perfect gift . . .

The next day, Lightning and Mater exchanged gifts.

"Open yours, open yours, open yours!" Mater cried.

"Okay," said Lightning. "But, Mater, I have some good news that . . ." Lightning trailed off as he unwrapped the tires.

"You got these for me?" he asked, looking up at his friend.

"Yeah!" Mater grinned from mirror to mirror. "If my best buddy can't be here for Christmas, then he'd sure as heck better win his Blushin' Mice Cup! Do you like 'em?"

Lightning was touched. "Mater, I love them. But . . ."

Mater was already ripping open his gift. When he saw the two tickets to Kersploosh Mountain, his eyes grew wide.

Lightning shrugged. "My race was delayed, so now I can spend Christmas with you, buddy."

"No way!" Mater exclaimed. "This is awesome! I can't believe we're going to Kersploosh Mountain on Christmas Day! Now we can take my sled and . . . uh-oh."

"Hey, where is your sled?" Lightning asked, looking around.

Mater shuffled nervously. "Uh, I may have kind of, sort of traded it to get you them there snow tires."

The two friends stared at each other. Then they started laughing. "Can you believe this?" Lightning exclaimed. "We thought we were getting each other the perfect Christmas presents, but we ended up getting stuff we can't use!"

Mater nodded. "Yeah, but I'll tell you one thing, buddy: spending Christmas together is still the best present ever."

Lightning smiled. "Same here, pal. I wouldn't change a thing."

Mater looked at the gifts. "Well, shoot. What are we going to do with four tires and no race, and two tickets with no sled?"

A twinkle came to Lightning's eye. "Well, we may not have a junkyard sled . . . but we do have a junkyard. Mater—didn't your old sled have *bumper tires?*"

Mater bounced up and down. "Oh, oh! I see where you're going." He started racing around his junkyard, collecting scraps. "Dad gum, this is gonna be so cool!"

On Christmas Day, Mater and Lightning sat at the top of
Kersploosh Mountain. Beneath them was a new junkyard sled.
Except this one was extra-special: it had two seats, flashing
Christmas lights, double gliders, and extra-large bumper tires.

"It's Mater's Junkyard Sled 0.2, with double the sledding fun!"
cried Mater.

"You ready for this?" Lightning asked as they teetered on the
top of the slide.

"You bet," said Mater. "As long as I've got my good buddy with
me, I'm as ready as I'll ever *beeeeeeeeeeee*!"

Wreck the Halls

Vanellope von Schweetz, president of Sugar Rush, lay down in
a drift of powdered sugar. "Ralph! Watch this!" she called to her
friend. Ralph was visiting from his own video game, Fix-It Felix, Jr.

Vanellope moved her arms and legs quickly through the fluffy
powder. Then she sprang to her feet. "Ta-da! A sugar angel!" she
exclaimed proudly.

Ralph smiled weakly. "Oh, yeah," he said. "Nice one."

Vanellope could tell something was bothering Ralph. "Hey! Shouldn't you be Mr. Holly Jolly? It's only a few days until Christmas—your first *real* Christmas!"

Christmastime was usually pretty lonely for video game Bad Guys like Ralph. But ever since Ralph had saved his game from being unplugged, the Nicelanders had realized what a good guy their Bad Guy was. This year, for the first time ever, they had even invited Ralph to their holiday party.

"It *was* great to go to the Nicelanders' party," Ralph told Vanellope. "But you know what? The whole time I was there, I couldn't stop thinking about the Bad Guys in all the other games. Their Christmases will be just as lonely as ever."

Ralph remembered past Christmases spent alone on his brick pile at the dump. "Bad Guys deserve a real Christmas, too," Ralph added.

Vanellope tilted her head to one side, then nodded. "You're right," she said. "And we can give it to them!" She remembered how it had felt to be left out by the other racers in her own game. "Let's throw the Bad Guys a Christmas party, with presents and a tree—the whole nine yards!"

Ralph's face lit up. "That's a perfect idea!" he cried. He hopped up in excitement, then landed with a *BOOM*! The ground shook and a towering sugar drift toppled over, burying Vanellope.

"Oops. Sorry," said Ralph, digging her out.

Ralph called a special meeting of the Bad-Anon support group.

"Every year, we Bad Guys get stuck on the outside of Christmas looking in. Well, this year, everything is going to be different!" Ralph told them all about how wonderful Christmas could be, with decorations, presents, songs, and parties. Everyone got really excited. Ralph's Christmas sounded like so much fun.

"I want everyone to meet here in the support group room on Christmas Eve," Ralph said. "And get ready for the merriest Christmas ever!"

Then Ralph and Vanellope got busy making a special gift for each Bad Guy. They planned something for everyone, including a new fireproof cape for Satine, eight cozy mittens for Cycloptopus, and a jar of extra-sticky taffy for Zombie—who was always looking for something to help reattach his arms.

"And now for the tree!" Vanellope declared. "It just isn't Christmas without a candy-covered tree."

They found a perfect lollipop tree in Lollistix Forest and cut it down. Then they strung it with popcorn garlands and hung candy canes from its branches. A glistening rock-candy star twinkled on top.

"Not bad!" Vanellope said, stepping back to admire it.

Ralph agreed. It didn't exactly look like the Nicelanders' Christmas tree, but he knew the Bad Guys would love it.

The presents were ready. The tree was ready. But with just one day left until Christmas Eve, Ralph was worried about something. "How are we going to carry all this to the support group room?"

Vanellope wrinkled her nose as she thought it over. Then her eyes widened. "The same way Santa does it!" she replied. "In a sleigh!"

Vanellope dragged Ralph across Sugar Rush to the kart bakery. There they could use all the sugar, frosting, and candy they needed to create the perfect Christmas kart.

"Has anyone ever made a sleigh here before?" Ralph asked.

"I doubt it!" Vanellope said as she fiddled with the controls. "But there's a first time for everything!"

Gears turned, belts rolled, mixers mixed, and frosting squirted.
Within minutes, a gleaming vehicle slid out of the finisher and came
to rest at Ralph's feet.

"One rocket-powered candy sleigh, ready to go!" Vanellope declared.

On Christmas Eve, the two friends met up to bring Christmas to the Bad Guys. Vanellope came dressed up and ready to play elf. "I didn't have a hat in size freakishly large, so I made you this." She tossed Ralph an empty sugar sack tied with a red bow on the side.

"Thanks!" said Ralph, putting it on. Then he squeezed behind the wheel of the rocket-powered sleigh. "Can I drive?"

"Uh . . . how about *I* get us off the ground?" Vanellope replied. She shooed Ralph into the passenger seat. "You can turn on the rockets once we get going." Vanellope revved the engines and they were off! Soon they were flying smoothly toward the game exit.

"Okay, let's get this thing moving!" Ralph called out, reaching for the left

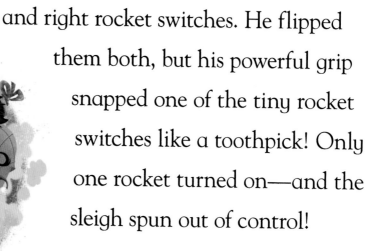

and right rocket switches. He flipped them both, but his powerful grip snapped one of the tiny rocket switches like a toothpick! Only one rocket turned on—and the sleigh spun out of control!

130

Vanellope tried to regain control of the runaway sleigh. First they zoomed left. Then they zipped right. But no matter what Vanellope did, it was no use! The rocket spiraled lower and lower until—*gloop!*—it came to a lurching stop in the middle of Great Caramel Lake.

Ralph and Vanellope managed to swim to shore, but the sleigh and all the presents were ruined. Ralph watched sadly as everything they had worked on sank beneath the caramel lake.

"Oh, no," he moaned.

Empty-handed and covered in caramel, Ralph and Vanellope made their way to the support group room. Ralph hesitated outside the door. "What are we going to tell the guys? I've wrecked their Christmas."

For once, Vanellope didn't have a snappy comeback. She knew the crash had been an accident, but she was still sad they wouldn't be able to have a Christmas party. "Time to face the music, big guy," she said, shaking her head.

But when they opened the door, the friends' jaws dropped.
The room was completely decked out—and the party was well
under way! The Bad Guys greeted them with a big cheer.

"Where did you get all this?" Ralph asked.

"We spent the last few days getting everything ready!"
Sorceress said.

"Yeah, you got us all in the Christmas spirit," Satine added.

"But Vanellope and I made presents, and trimmed a tree. . . . We even made a sleigh, but I wrecked it. I wrecked everything."

"Don't be silly, Ralph!" said Satine. "You're the reason we're here—spending the holiday together!" The other Bad Guys nodded in agreement. "That's a pretty great gift."

Vanellope punched Ralph gently on the arm. "Yeah, don't be silly, Ralph," she said. "Or should I say 'Mr. Holly Jolly'?"

A wide smile spread across Ralph's face. "That's me!" he exclaimed. "Merry Christmas, everyone!" And as they all celebrated late into the night, it truly was the merriest Christmas any of them had ever had.

Christmas Laughs

Mike Wazowski, the green one-eyed monster, was on the Monsters, Inc. Laugh Floor. He couldn't keep from looking at the Laugh Meter. It showed all of the laughs the monsters had collected by telling kids jokes. The laughs were turned into energy for the city of Monstropolis.

Monsters, Inc. had always been able to collect enough laughs to make sure the monsters never had to worry about losing power. But with Christmas around the corner, it seemed as if more and more kids were on vacation. That made it harder to collect laughs.

Mike worried that there wouldn't be enough power to light up the Christmas tree in the city center. It was a Monstropolis tradition that everyone looked forward to.

"Come on, monsters," he called out. "Think funny!"

Mike watched one monster go through a child's closet door. When he came back onto the Laugh Floor, Mike looked at the canister that collected laughs. It wasn't even half full.

Just then, Sulley showed up. The big, furry blue monster
was the president of Monsters, Inc. He was also Mike's best friend.
"How's it going, Mike?" asked Sulley.
"Fine, fine," Mike answered nervously. He didn't want his boss
to know they were running short on laughs. "That
Christmas tree will be lit up in no time."
Mike saw Sulley peek over at the
Laugh Meter. "I bet there are a lot of
kids who are—" Sulley started.
"No time to talk, buddy,"
Mike cut him off. He guided
Sulley toward the door. "Got to
get back to work and collect
those laughs."
"Okay," said Sulley.
"See you later."

As soon as Sulley left, Mike called out again, "Let's go, let's go! Collect those laughs! Christmas is just around the corner!"

The monsters worked even harder at being funny and entertaining. One monster even juggled seven plates and spun another plate on his head. The kid watching him broke into giggles and clapped wildly. The laugh canister quickly filled up.

George, a big, furry orange monster, went through another child's door. He sat on a stool next to the little girl's bed, holding a microphone in one hand.

"Hey, is this thing on? Hello?" George said, tapping the microphone. "Ready to have some laughs? Good. Why did the monster eat a lightbulb?"

"Why?" the child asked.

"He needed a light snack!" George exclaimed, and the little girl roared with laughter. "Wait, wait! I have more." He told another joke that sent the child into giggles. On the Laugh Floor, Mike watched the canister outside the door fill up.

"Nice work," Mike said when George had finished.

"Thanks," George said. He and Mike looked up at the Laugh Meter on the wall. It was growing steadily, much to everyone's delight.

"We actually might make our goal," Mike said with a hopeful smile.

All of a sudden, Mike and the other monsters watched in horror as the Laugh Meter began to go *down* instead of up!

"What's going on? What's happening?" Mike said, his voice growing louder.

The laugh wranglers, Smitty and Needleman, weren't sure.

"This has never happened before," said Smitty, the head wrangler.

"Well, don't just stand there," Mike cried. *"Fix it!"*

The wranglers sprang into action. After a while, they discovered a leak in the laugh tank, where all the laughs were stored.

The monsters on the Laugh Floor were worried. They wondered if all of their hard work had been for nothing.

"Ho, ho, ho!" came a cheerful voice.

Mike looked up and saw Santa Claus walking onto the floor. Then he realized it was Sulley dressed in a Santa suit.

"I'm just getting into the Christmas spirit," Sulley explained. Then he looked around. "It looks like I'm the only one. What's going on?"

Mike explained the problem. "But I've got everything under control, Santa, er, Sulley."

"I'm sure you do," Sulley replied. "I'm just going to see if there's anything I can do to help."

Sulley followed Mike into the basement of Monsters, Inc., where the laugh wranglers were hard at work. Everyone wanted to get the laugh tank fixed as soon as possible, and time was running out. The tree-lighting ceremony was only a few hours away!

But the wranglers couldn't agree on how to fix the problem.

"Anything I can do?" Sulley asked.

"One of the pipes that leads into the laugh tank has burst," explained Smitty. "We need to tie it off, but none of our tools are strong enough to turn the pipe."

"Hmm . . . " said Sulley, scratching his head.

Then Mike had a great idea. "Why not actually *tie it off*?" Since Sulley was so strong, he could bend that pipe right into a pretzel shape!

Sulley was willing to give it a try. Mike stood by his side and coached him.

It worked! The pipe stopped leaking!

Mike and Sulley headed back up to the Laugh Floor. All the monsters congratulated Sulley!

Mike wondered why no one was thanking *him*. It had been his idea, after all. But there was no time to think about that now. "We're back up and running!" Mike announced. "Let's make some laughs!"

All the monsters got to work. They knew they'd have to work extra hard to make up for all the lost laughs.

Sulley decided to jump in and help. "Hey, we've only got a couple hours to get the tree lit," he said to Mike.

Still dressed as Santa, Sulley went through a child's closet door.

When he came back onto the Laugh Floor, he looked up at the Laugh Meter on the wall. It was increasing, but slowly.

"We've got to make it," Sulley whispered to Mike.

Finally, the Laugh Meter was back up to the level it had reached before the leak. Sulley looked at the clock on the wall and frowned. It was only thirty minutes until the tree-lighting ceremony.

Suddenly, Sulley had an idea. "The only way we're going to make our laugh quota is to get some really over-the-top laughs."

Mike nodded in agreement.

"We need a grand slam here," continued Sulley. "We need a special kind of monster. One with perfect timing . . . star quality . . . a natural at comedy . . . a one-eyed sensation."

Mike realized what Sulley was trying to do. He crossed his arms and shook his head. "No, Sulley. Absolutely not."

"The Christmas tree lighting is only half an hour away," Sulley told him. "Come on, Mike. The whole city is depending on you."

That was all Mike needed to hear. "You're right. Let's do it!" he said. "But *you're* coming with me!"

Sulley and Mike went through a door together. Sulley was still dressed as Santa, and Mike had dressed up as an elf. To their delight, a little girls' sleepover was going on!

Mike started with some of his best jokes. "Hey, Sulley, I've got to walk twenty-five miles to get home."

"Why don't you take a train?" Sulley asked, playing along.

"I did once, but my mother made me give it back!" Mike said.

The kids in the room laughed, but not as hard as the monsters had hoped. After a few more jokes, Mike realized he'd have to try something else. He picked up the sack of toys Sulley had brought in, but it was far too heavy for him.

"*Whoa!!*" he exclaimed as he tripped. He landed upside down, and the sack of toys spilled out around him. He sat up with a doll draped over his head and a toy race car stuck to his foot.

The kids roared with laughter. They begged for more, and Mike happily tumbled and tripped for them again.

Mike and Sulley made it back onto the Laugh Floor in time to watch the Laugh Meter hit its limit!

At the tree-lighting ceremony, Mike and Sulley stood proudly in the front of the crowd.

Sulley leaned over and whispered in Mike's ear, "You did a great job. Thank you."

Mike smiled. "You know what I always say: funny doesn't grow on trees. When you got it, you got it. And I got it."

Sulley laughed. He was happy Mike had it—and shared it. It was going to be a bright Christmas, after all.

The Holiday Treasure Hunt

Ariel and her husband, Prince Eric, were walking along the beach. It was only a few days before Christmas, but the weather was still mild. Suddenly, Eric's dog, Max, ran up to them. He was carrying a waterlogged boot.

"I've been searching for that boot for months!" cried Eric.

"Burying things and digging them up is Max's favorite game," said Ariel, shaking her head. It looked like Eric needed a new pair of boots. At least now Ariel knew what to give him for Christmas! But she had only a few days to think of gifts for everyone else.

Ariel and Eric returned to the castle. As soon as they stepped inside, Carlotta, the housekeeper, announced it was time for tea.

"Already?" asked Grimsby, the butler, checking his pocket watch. He gave it a tap. "Hmm . . . must be broken."

Eric and Ariel invited Grimsby and Carlotta to join them for some tasty treats beside the Christmas tree.

"Isn't the tree beautiful?" Ariel remarked. "Carlotta suggested we use red and gold decorations this year."

"Why, thank you," Carlotta replied. "Those are my favorite colors, you know."

Ariel was delighted. Now she had gift ideas for Carlotta and Grimsby!

The next day, Ariel went into town to do her Christmas shopping. There she found the perfect pair of boots for Eric. For a special surprise, she also got a bottle with a tiny little ship built inside. It reminded Ariel of the first time she met Eric—beside his ship.

Then she chose a shiny pocket watch for Grimsby. The trusty timepiece would certainly help him keep everything on schedule. At the jewelry store, Ariel searched for something in Carlotta's favorite colors. Soon she bought a gold necklace with a ruby pendant. Max's present was easy. Ariel stopped at a butcher shop and got the biggest bone she could find!

Ariel still had to find gifts for her father, her sisters, and her friends from the sea. When she saw a shop window filled with colorful glass hearts, she knew her search was over. "What beautiful ornaments," Ariel told the shopkeeper. "I'll take them all!"

Back at the castle, Ariel carefully wrapped the gifts and wrote
a special message for each one. She finished the last note and
attached it to King Triton's present. But when
she placed her father's gift on the pile of
wrapped presents, she realized something
was missing. It was Max's gift. Suddenly,
Ariel heard a loud chewing noise coming
from behind a chair. Max was gnawing
happily on the bone she had gotten for
him.

"No opening presents early, Max!"
Ariel scolded. She took the bone
from Max and hid it
and the other
presents under
the bed.

On Christmas morning, everyone at the castle shared a festive holiday breakfast.

Afterward, Ariel went to her room to get everyone's gifts. But when she looked under her bed, all the gifts were gone! She looked under the rug. Then she checked inside the closet. She even looked behind the curtains, but the gifts were nowhere to be found.

"Ariel!" Eric called upstairs. "It's time for presents!"

Ariel joined the prince by the tree. "Is it all right if we do that later? I told my merfamily and friends I'd meet them on the beach this morning." Ariel decided she could keep looking for the presents later.

"Of course," replied Eric. "Come along, everyone. We're going on a Christmas visit."

Ariel's friends Flounder, Sebastian, and Scuttle were waiting on the beach. Scuttle the seagull handed Ariel a small chest. "We thought these whatchamajinglys would come in handy!"

Ariel opened the lid and saw the sorts of treasures she had loved to collect when she was a mermaid. There was a bent fork and a cracked mirror. "Thank you!"

"We all helped find them," Flounder said proudly.

Just then, King Triton and Ariel's sisters swam up.

"Merry Christmas!" they called.

"Merry Christmas!" Ariel replied, waving to her family.

"We brought presents!" Ariel's sister Aquata shouted.

"Oh, thank you!" Ariel exclaimed. "I have gifts for all of you, too, except—"

"Woof! Woof!" Max barked. The dog ran up, holding a boot.

"Your present!" Ariel said to Eric. Now she knew where the missing gifts were. Max had buried them on the beach!

Ariel thought quickly. "Surprise, everyone! We're going on a Christmas-gift treasure hunt!"

"Ariel, you are amazing!" Eric said. "Only you could turn the holidays into a new adventure."

Soon Eric, Carlotta, Max, and Grimsby were digging around on the beach.

Ariel's friends and merfamily cheered them on.

"Try digging near the old rowboat!" Flounder said.

"Or near that sand castle!" Aquata shouted.

Each time someone discovered a present, Scuttle would pick it up and deliver it to the right person.

"First Class Airmail for Carlotta!" Scuttle called as he dropped a small package in the housekeeper's lap.

The treasure hunt was loud, sandy, and the most fun anyone could remember having on Christmas morning. Everyone loved Ariel's gifts.

After the treasure hunt was over, everyone gathered by the water's edge to say good-bye.

"Merry Christmas!" they called to each other, as Ariel and Eric headed back to the castle.

Inside, the pair sat by the fire and admired their gifts. "What a wonderful holiday tradition," Eric said. "We should have a Christmas treasure hunt every year!"

Ariel just smiled. It had been a day full of surprises, and sometimes the most unexpected treasures were the best.

Finding Nemo

A Big Blue Christmas

"Dad, wake up!" Nemo shouted early one morning as he swam back and forth across their anemone home.

"What is it, Nemo?" asked Marlin, waking in a hurry. "Are you hurt? Is something wrong?"

"No, Dad," the little clownfish answered. "It's just that I have a terrific idea! It's almost Christmas. Could we have a holiday party?"

"Sounds like fun, Nemo," Marlin said with a yawn. "But let's wait until after breakfast to start planning."

Right after breakfast, Nemo
and Marlin made a list of
friends to invite. It was a long
list because they had friends
all over the ocean. Marlin
wondered how they'd let
everyone know in time.

"I can ask Bruce, Chum,
and Anchor to help spread the
word," Nemo offered. "No one
can say 'no' to those guys."

Marlin thought it over. Nemo
was right. No fish he knew wanted to get on a shark's
bad side. "Well, all right, son," he said. "But be careful."

"I know, Dad," Nemo said. "See you later!" he called as
he swam off.

Nemo swam as fast as he could to the old shipwreck where his shark friends hung out. "Hey, Bruce! Guys!" Nemo said when he arrived.

"Check out what the tide washed in," said Anchor.

"Why it's our little food—I mean, friend—Nemo," Chum said.

"What brings you out this way, Nemo?" asked Bruce.

The little clownfish told them all about the Christmas party. The sharks were thrilled. They hadn't been invited to many parties. Then Nemo asked them to help tell everyone about it.

"You can count on us," Bruce said proudly.

"Thanks," said Nemo. "And, guys, we will be counting our guests, too, so remember . . ."

"Fish are friends, not food," the four of them said together.

Nemo swam home as fast as he could. His father was swimming back and forth across their anemone nervously.

"We need to plan the menu," Marlin muttered. "And then there's cleaning and decorating and . . ."

"Stop right there, Dad," said Nemo. "We're going to need help. I'll be back later with more fins!"

Nemo had made some great friends when he had been captured and put in a tank in a dentist's office. The whole Tank Gang had eventually escaped and were now living in the ocean. Nemo went to find them and ask for their help with the party.

When Nemo returned home that afternoon, two of his old pals from the Tank Gang were with him.

Deb was a blue-and-white humbug fish. She got to work on the food. But she insisted on keeping the dessert a surprise.

Jacques was a tiny cleaner shrimp. Jacques started to work doing what he did best: cleaning. Soon the anemone was so clean it sparkled.

"It's too bad Flo couldn't be here," said Deb sadly. "She does like a party."

Nemo and Marlin winked at each other. They knew that Flo was really only Deb's reflection in the tank glass.

Next Nemo swam off to find their friend Dory, the regal blue tang fish.

"Do I know you?" Dory asked when Nemo finally found her. Nemo smiled. Dory was the most forgetful fish he knew. All of a sudden, Dory hugged him and said, "Memo! I've missed you!"

"Would you like to help us decorate for a party?" said Nemo.

"I *love* parties," said Dory. "At least I think I love parties. I can't really remember if I've ever been to one."

That afternoon, Dory, Marlin, and Nemo worked hard putting up all the decorations. They hung streamers and wreaths and decorated a conch-shell Christmas tree.

Meanwhile, the sharks were busy inviting all the guests. Finally, just the sea turtles were left. The three sharks took a ride on the East Australian Current to catch up with them.

"Hey, shark dudes," Crush said. "What's happening?"

"Nemo and Marlin asked us to invite you to a holiday party back at their anemone," Bruce said.

"Awesome," said Crush. "I love to party!"

Squirt popped out from underneath Crush's back flipper. "Hey, dudes, can I come, too?"

"Of course," said Chum. "Nemo wants all his foods—I mean, friends—there."

"Cool!" said Squirt.

Back at the anemone, there was only one more detail left to plan. A good party needed great music. That gave Nemo an idea.

Nemo went to see his friends Tad the butterfly fish, Sheldon the sea horse, and Pearl the squid.

"Hi, Nemo," said Sheldon.

"Hi, guys," Nemo said. "Guess what? My dad and I are having a holiday party. But we need a band. I thought we could play!"

"Cool," said Pearl. "I've been humming 'Jingle Shells' all day!"

"Let's practice right now," added Tad. He grabbed some kelp and started to strum.

Pearl joined in on the sand-dollar tambourines. Sheldon kept the beat on the clams.

Then Nemo joined in on the conch shell on the second verse. They practiced all afternoon.

"We'll be great!" Nemo said when they finished. They sounded really good. "See you at the party!"

Finally, the night of the party arrived! Wearing colorful Christmas sea garlands, Marlin and Nemo greeted their guests. Seeing all of his friends together filled Nemo with holiday cheer.

"Welcome to our party," Marlin said to Crush and Squirt.

"Merry Christmas!" Nemo said to Dory and the sharks.

"Thanks," said Dory as she swam past. "I just ran into these guys, and they told me there was a party over here tonight. Hey, these decorations look amazing. Who did them?"

"Dory, you helped me decorate for the party," Nemo said.

"I did?" asked Dory. "Wow, I'm good."

Before long, the party was filled with friends from near and far. Deb's seaweed-and-kelp cake was delicious. There was even a ginger-kelp fish decorating the top of the cake. Everyone loved that best of all. The guests washed their treats down with salty seawater punch. Everyone was gathered around the conch-shell Christmas tree having a great time.

"Time to open presents!" announced Marlin. He swam over to the conch-shell tree.

Dory swam around the other guests muttering, "Where is that present I brought? Wait, did I bring a present? Whose birthday is it anyway?"

All around Nemo, his friends were opening presents and thanking each other. But Nemo was most excited about watching Bubbles open the gift he'd gotten for him. The yellow tang fish was another one of his old friends from the tank at the dentist's office.

"Open it, Bubbles, open it!" Nemo urged.

Inside, Bubbles found a brand-new tiny treasure chest. When he opened the top, a cloud of bubbles came out.

Bubbles giggled. "How I've missed my bubbles! Thank you, Nemo."

The little treasure chest was one of the few things any of them missed from their days living in the tank. Nemo had found it on the ocean floor during a trip with his father. He'd known that it was the perfect gift for Bubbles.

After all the presents were opened, Nemo decided it was time for some live music.

"C'mon, guys," Nemo whispered to Pearl, Sheldon, and Tad. "Time to get everyone singing and dancing."

And they did! The guests all turned to watch as Nemo, Sheldon, Tad, and Pearl started to play "We Wish You a Merry Fishmas."

Mr. Ray, Nemo's teacher, sang along loudly. Even the sharks flipped their fins to the beat.

The party really got swinging as the band played more Christmas carols.

In between songs, Deb swam over to Nemo. "Great party," Deb said. "Your dad is such a nice guy. Isn't it wonderful being able to travel the big wide ocean to visit friends?"

"You bet, Deb!" Nemo answered. He slapped fins with his friend. "Fish aren't meant to live in a tank."

It was getting late
and soon the guests
began to swim home,
calling out "Merry
Christmas" and
"Happy New Year"
as they left.

When the last of
the guests had gone,
Nemo turned to his
father and smiled.
"Dad, this was the
best Christmas ever."

"You bet it was," said Marlin. "We sure are lucky to have so
many good friends. But the best gift of all is spending Christmas
with you." And he gave his son a big hug.

Lady's Christmas Surprise

It was the week before Christmas. Tramp and the puppies gathered beneath Jim and Darling's brightly decorated tree.

"You all know what holiday is coming up, right?" Tramp asked, his eyes twinkling.

"Of course, Dad," Scamp said. He was excited. Christmas was the puppies' favorite holiday. Lots of guests stopped by to wish Jim and Darling a happy holiday.

But the best part was the presents. The puppies got to help choose a special gift for each of their parents. They loved being trusted with two such important surprises.

"Do any of you kids know what your mother would like for Christmas?" Tramp asked.

"How about a steak from Tony's Restaurant?" Annette said.

Tramp shook his head. "We can do better than that."

"We need to give her something special," said Colette, "to show how much we love her."

"Why don't you ask her what she'd like?" said Scamp, his voice muffled. He was chewing on a bow.

"We want to surprise her," Tramp reminded his son. He nudged him away from the presents. "That's the fun of Christmas."

"Maybe we'll find something on our walk today," Annette said.

Tramp thought that was a good idea. While Lady was taking a nap, he took the kids into town to look for the perfect present.

The village bustled with shoppers, their carriage wheels carving deep ruts in the snowy road.

The dogs rambled up and down the avenue, looking in all the shop windows. They saw sweaters, cushions, brush and comb sets, bowls, and collars. But Tramp knew that none of these things was the perfect gift for Lady. He wanted to find her something special. Something that she would enjoy and that no other dog would have.

Tramp and the puppies kept looking into store windows and they peeked at the packages people carried. All they needed was one really good idea.

When the sun started to sink in the sky, Tramp turned to the puppies and said, "We'd better head home now. Maybe we'll find something tomorrow."

As they crossed the road, Tramp noticed something sparkling in the snow. It was much brighter than an icicle. He turned it over with his paw.

"Holy hambones!" he cried. It was a gold and emerald necklace!

"What a bunch of rocks!" exclaimed Scamp.

"What a good stroke of luck!" remarked Annette.

"Just the right size for Mother!" added Colette.

Tramp smiled and then scooped up the necklace with his mouth. It seemed they'd found the perfect gift. He knew it would look beautiful on Lady.

At that moment, a woman rushed into the station. "Help!" she cried. "My necklace is gone! I'm offering a reward for its return."

The policeman smiled at the woman. Then he held out the necklace. "Is this yours?" he asked. He pointed to Tramp. "This dog found it on the street and brought it here."

The woman gasped. "Thank you," she said. She scratched Tramp behind his ear. "How can I repay you?"

Woof! Tramp looked at the necklace.

"A new collar," she said. "That's it!"

She took Tramp and the puppies to the shop next door. Tramp walked up to the counter and picked up a gold collar with green stones that looked just like the woman's necklace.

"I'll take that one," the woman told the shopkeeper.

On Christmas morning Lady tore open the gift. "You shouldn't have!" Her eyes sparkled like the green stones.

When Darling fastened the collar around Lady's neck, she pranced around the room as if she were a show dog.

"I love my new collar," Lady said. "What a wonderful Christmas surprise! But I love my family even more." She nuzzled Tramp and each of the puppies.

"Merry Christmas, Mother," said the puppies.

And it was a very merry Christmas, indeed.

THE PRINCESS AND THE FROG

The Christmas Feast

Princess Tiana and Prince Naveen were celebrating their first Christmas together. Tiana had invited their family and friends to her restaurant for a Christmas Eve feast. She wanted Naveen to share in the traditions she knew and loved.

"We might need to buy more ornaments," Tiana said.

"As long as they're fit for a princess!" Naveen replied. That week he had helped Tiana decorate her restaurant, make centerpieces, and put up a tree— but there was still more work to be done.

Tiana needed to buy ingredients for Christmas Eve dinner. So she and Naveen headed to the market.

"I can't wait to taste the feast you're going to make," Naveen said. "With my help, of course!"

"Well, we need quite a few things," Tiana said. "Let's see. First we should get the vegetables."

Tiana carefully looked through all the produce at the vegetable stall. She wanted to make sure she had all the freshest ingredients for their Christmas feast.

Next was the butcher shop, and then they stopped for some eggs and cheese. Finally, all Tiana needed was some powdered sugar for her famous beignets.

"I think we'll have to make another trip," said Naveen as he struggled with a tower of parcels. "How many people are we cooking for?"

"My mother, Charlotte, Big Daddy, your parents, and our friends from the town and the bayou. We'll be serving as many people as want to join us," Tiana said happily. "After all, the more the merrier!"

Tiana spent the next few days cooking and baking with
Naveen by her side. "For someone who didn't know how to chop a
mushroom, you've become quite an expert," Tiana told Naveen.

"You taught me everything I know," Naveen reminded her.

When darkness fell on Christmas Eve, all the food for the banquet was finally ready.

"Before our guests arrive, I have a surprise for you," Tiana announced, handing Naveen his coat.

"Where are we going?" he asked.

"You'll find out soon enough," Tiana answered mysteriously.

"Just a hint?" Naveen pleaded.

But Tiana simply smiled silently.

Tiana walked Naveen to the riverside and, together, they paddled a canoe into the bayou. As they turned a corner, Naveen's surprise came into view: there were huge bonfires burning alongside the river.

"The fires are for Papa Noel," Tiana explained.

"So he can find his way in the sky?" asked Naveen.

Tiana laughed. "Papa Noel doesn't use a sleigh. He travels in a pirogue. That's a flat-bottomed canoe, pulled by alligators."

"I hope he leaves the gators outside when he delivers the presents!" Naveen exclaimed.

Fog rolled in, and Tiana and Naveen paddled toward home. The folks along the river pointed excitedly at the couple's canoe. Through the mist, all they could see was the couple's red blanket. "Look!" the river folk shouted. "It's him!" They thought Tiana and Naveen's canoe belonged to Papa Noel! All around them, people jumped into their boats and paddled behind the canoe, hoping to catch a glimpse of the mysterious visitor.

When the bayou folk paddled out of the fog, they found Tiana and Naveen standing on the dock.

"Have you seen Papa Noel?" someone asked.

"We haven't, but since you're in town, would you join us for dinner? There's plenty to share!" Tiana said.

"Thank you," said one of the travelers. "I guess we don't mind if we do!"

By the time Tiana and Naveen reached Tiana's Palace, guests were starting to arrive.

Tiana greeted Naveen's parents and her mother, Eudora. She welcomed her best friend, Charlotte, and her friend's father, Big Daddy LaBouff.

"Some of the guests are saying they saw Papa Noel on the river," Charlotte said. "Do you suppose that's him there?"

Tiana looked up and saw an elderly man in a red suit with the other guests.

She was curious, but she had to finish cooking and put on her party dress.

In the dining room, Tiana's alligator friend, Louis, handed out parcels of sugared fruits and candy. Each box was wrapped with shiny purple paper and topped with a beautiful golden bow.

One woman was especially excited to see Louis. "It's one of Papa Noel's alligators!" the woman said.

Louis gave her a wide, toothy smile. It was nice that none of the guests were afraid of him!

Soon Tiana and Naveen brought out the food.

"Dinner is served!" Tiana announced. Everyone cheered when they saw the table full of food. There were pots of Tiana's delicious gumbo, turkey with chestnuts, roasted ham, grits, yams, vegetables, and soufflés.

The guests heaped their plates high and dug in.

Tiana smiled. There was nothing she liked better than friends enjoying her cooking.

Some of the guests ate second, third, and even forth helpings!

After everyone had eaten, Naveen and Louis played jazzy versions of their favorite Christmas carols. Tiana invited her guests to dance to the music.

Snow fell quietly on the kingdom of Arendelle.

The town was blanketed in white. Snowflakes tickled children's noses and melted on their tongues. The people of Arendelle waded through deep, powdery snowdrifts as they hurried through the streets. Everyone welcomed the snow, for this time it was not Queen Elsa's doing. It was winter, and Christmas was coming!

DISNEY
FROZEN

All I Want for Christmas

Just then, Naveen walked up. "What a wonderful dinner!" he exclaimed. "The food! The music! The people! It's all so . . ."

"Wonderful? It *is* Christmastime in New Orleans." Then Tiana spotted the man in the red suit. "Do you think that's Papa Noel?"

Before Tiana could investigate, Naveen led her onto the dance floor. "Stranger things have happened," he said.

Tiana grinned. She was delighted that Naveen's first New Orleans Christmas was going so well—for her, that was magic enough.

As the band finished off another toe-tapping tune, Tiana realized she had forgotten to serve desert! Quickly, she ran to the kitchen and filled a cart with custards, cakes, and beignets. The cart was so full that Tiana could barely open the kitchen door.

"Let me help you with that, my dear," said a white-bearded gentleman. He helped Tiana push the cart into the dining room. As Tiana ducked back into the kitchen, she realized the man looked just like Papa Noel! Tiana hurried back to the dining room, but the man had already vanished.

Inside the castle, Queen Elsa couldn't wait for Christmas. This year, everything would be different. For the first time since Elsa was a child, the kingdom's gates were open. Elsa's ice magic was finally under control. And most importantly, Elsa and her sister, Anna, were friends again.

Elsa hadn't had a merry Christmas in a long time. Worse, her little sister hadn't, either. Elsa felt terrible about that. Anna was the most important person in her life, but Elsa had been cold and distant to her for years and years. Now Elsa wanted to make up for lost time.

This year, Elsa was going to make sure that Anna had the merriest Christmas ever.

Elsa got started the very next day.

"Kristoff!" she called as she spotted her sister's friend crossing the castle courtyard. "I need your help."

Elsa explained her plan to create the perfect Christmas for Anna. "I thought you and I could make an ice sculpture for her," Elsa said.

So Kristoff and Elsa locked the ballroom door and got to work on a beautiful sculpture of Anna.

"Elsa?" Anna called. She knocked on the door. "Are you in there?"

"Don't come in!" Elsa cried. "It's a surprise!"

Next Elsa found Olaf and told the snowman about her plan.

"I've got the perfect idea!" Olaf cheered. "Let's bake Anna some Christmas cookies!"

Elsa was a little skeptical. "I'm not sure you should go anywhere near an oven."

"Pshaw!" Olaf said, waving his twiggy arms. "What could possibly go wrong?"

So Olaf and Elsa got to work. Elsa decided to make extra-gingery gingerbread men. The cookies turned out perfectly, and Elsa only had to refreeze Olaf seven times.

"Elsa?" Anna said from behind kitchen door. "It smells great in there! Can I help?"

"Nope!" Elsa called back. "It's a surprise! I'll see you later, okay?"

Kristoff's reindeer, Sven, didn't talk much. Well, he didn't talk at all. (After all, he was a reindeer.) But Elsa explained her plan to him anyway, and he seemed to understand.

"I want this Christmas tree to be glitzy," Elsa said, "but still tasteful."

Sven nodded his

head very, very carefully. The ornaments on his antlers clinked together softly. Elsa hung another glass ball on the tree.

"Anna will love it," Elsa told him. "She's going to be so happy!"

Elsa worked and worked. She kept thinking of new things to do to make Anna's Christmas even more perfect. She drew frost snowflakes on windowpanes. She hired musicians to play Christmas carols throughout the castle. She hung evergreen wreaths on every door.

Soon a cheery fire burned in every fireplace in the castle. There were piles of treats on every table. The entire castle glittered with decorations, ice sculptures, and tinsel. And the closets were stuffed with presents covered in brightly colored wrapping paper.

Elsa paused for a moment to admire her handiwork. Everything looked beautiful, but it still wasn't *perfect*. "Where's Anna?" Kristoff asked as he walked in to check the ice sculpture. "I haven't seen her for a while."

"Oh," Elsa said, "I told her to stay in her room so the surprise wouldn't be ruined."

"Hmmm," Kristoff said with a frown. "You know, Elsa, I think what Anna would really like is—"

"Some Christmas punch!" Elsa finished his sentence for him. "You're right! We don't have any punch!" She bustled out of the room.

"I was going to say, 'to spend some time with her big sister,'" Kristoff said to the empty room.

Elsa was stirring a big bowl of punch when Anna walked into the kitchen. She quickly hid the ladle behind her back.

"What are you doing outside of your room?" Elsa asked.

"It's boring in there," Anna said. "And lonely. I'd rather hang out with you."

"But you'll ruin your surprise!"

Anna rolled her eyes. "I have a surprise for you, too," she said, walking out of the kitchen. "Follow me."

Elsa followed Anna outside to a snowy courtyard—but Anna
had disappeared!

"Anna? Where are you?" Elsa called. "I don't have time for this.
There are still a million things I need to—"

Splat! A snowball hit Elsa right in the face.

"Surprise!" Anna yelled.

"W–what?" Elsa sputtered, brushing snow off her face. "Did you just—?"

"It's a snowball intervention, Elsa," Anna said dramatically. "Since you don't seem to have any time for me, I'm declaring war!"

Elsa started to grin. "Anna," she said, "I think you're forgetting

which one of us has magical ice powers." She made a huge snowball and hurled it at Anna.

The snowball fight lasted for hours, until the sisters were too tired to go on. They hurried inside and sat down in Elsa's overdecorated room.

"Now, what did we learn today?" Anna asked with a smirk.

"I'm sorry I ignored you," Elsa said. "I got carried away with making your Christmas perfect, and I forgot all about the most important part—spending time with you."

"It's all lovely," Anna reassured her. "And it was really sweet of you to do it. But for me, the best Christmas present ever is just being with you."

The two sisters sat quietly by the fire. After a while, Anna fell asleep with her head on Elsa's shoulder.

"For me, too," Elsa whispered. "Merry Christmas."

Christmas for Everyone

On Christmas Eve, a brave fox named Robin Hood and his bear friend Little John were celebrating in Sherwood Forest.

They had roasted a goose and some chestnuts over an open fire.

"A true feast!" said Friar Tuck, a badger, when he saw the goose. He knelt beside the fire to warm his hands.

"We did our best," said Little John. "It wasn't easy to get a bird on Christmas Eve. But good ol' Rob knows where to find things." He chuckled.

Robin Hood laughed. "Johnny, you give me too much credit. The goose was a Christmas gift from the Sheriff of Nottingham. He won't miss one little bird. You should see the spread he's got over there."

"I'm sure," Friar Tuck said. "He won't notice a missing goose when he's already got a chicken and a turkey on his holiday table." Friar Tuck shook his head. "Doesn't seem right. That old Sheriff gets more greedy by the day. By the hour!"

Robin Hood thought about what Friar Tuck had said. When they sat down to dinner with Toby Turtle and Allan-a-Dale the rooster, Robin noticed everyone looked a little down.

"This isn't a cheerful Christmas feast," Little John noted.

"Something's not right," said Toby Turtle.

Robin Hood nodded. He knew Toby was right, but he couldn't figure out what the problem was either.

"The goose tastes great," Toby said. "It's just that . . ."

"Would some Christmas music lighten the mood?" Allan-a-Dale asked as he picked up his guitar.

"I know what it is, Robin," Little John said. He looked sad. "We took the day off to get ready for Christmas. The only thing we stole was . . ."

"The goose!" Robin Hood cried. He couldn't believe he hadn't thought of all the poor people of Nottingham who didn't have anything to eat this Christmas holiday.

"The poor people of Nottingham don't have anything to eat?" Friar Tuck asked.

He felt terrible. All day, he'd gone around to the poorest families handing out small purses full of coins gathered from the collection plate. He hadn't thought to bring a Christmas feast to anyone. A single tear rolled down his cheek.

"A Christmas feast is an important part of the holiday," said

Robin. "And I think I know where we can find one at this late hour."

Little John smiled. "Who deserves a feast the least?" he crowed. He knew exactly what Robin was thinking.

"The Sheriff of Nottingham!" Toby said.

The friends set off through the forest on their sleigh. They were on their way to the sheriff's house. They knew he would have plenty of food to spare.

When they reached the sheriff's home, they peered through the frosted window. Robin gasped at the sight before them. A Yule log blazed on the hearth. The tree twinkled with candles, and gifts were everywhere. Steam rose from the large dining table.

"Look at all those gifts, all that food. I can think of a dozen families who would be grateful for just one item from that pile," Robin Hood said to Little John. "I'll go to the front door and distract the sheriff. Johnny, you take the men inside, bring the feast and presents out through the kitchen. Then load up the sleigh."

Robin quickly disguised himself as a blind beggar and rapped on the sheriff's door. When the sheriff opened it, Robin said, "Alms for a poor blind man on this wintry eve?"

"Oh, you beggars!" the sheriff said. "Can't you give it a rest? It's Christmas Eve, and I'm trying to eat my dinner in peace."

The sheriff went to close the door, but Robin held it open.

"All the more reason to spare something, kind sir," Robin said.

"Now wait just a minute there," the sheriff said. "Haven't I seen that outfit before?"

Robin Hood shook his head.

The Sheriff lunged forward to grab the beggar. Robin ducked, but the sheriff caught his arm. He lifted the hat on the beggar's head and saw the smiling face of Robin Hood!

"I knew it!" the sheriff said as he looked at Robin. "You can't fool the good Sheriff of Nottingham."

Robin smiled. He had tricked the sheriff plenty of times before.

He wriggled free of the sheriff's grip and ran off. The sheriff chased him into Sherwood Forest. Robin laughed as he ran. He was so quick that the sheriff could hardly keep up!

When Robin had put enough distance between himself and the sheriff, he climbed high into a tree. He carefully creeped out onto a thick branch to watch for the sheriff. He knew the evil man wouldn't give up easily.

Robin heard footsteps crunching through the snow. He peered down and watched the sheriff run through the woods calling after him. The sheriff searched for Robin, but he couldn't find even a footprint.

"I'll get you this time, Robin Hood!" the sheriff called as he ran.

Robin chuckled as he slid to the ground. He'd bested the sheriff once again.

Meanwhile, Little John and the rest of the men had taken the sheriff's gifts and feast. They loaded their sleigh with brightly wrapped packages, roast turkey, and plum pudding. They even took the magnificent Christmas tree.

Little John took hold of the front of the sleigh and started to run. Robin Hood soon caught up with his friends. "There's no time to waste," he said. "The sheriff is mad. We've got to get these gifts delivered before he takes them all back!"

Maid Marian, a kind young fox, and her lady-in-waiting, a cheerful hen named Lady Kluck, passed by the sleigh in their carriage.

"Why, Robin Hood, what a merry surprise!" Marian said as the carriage pulled to a stop.

Robin bowed low to the ladies. "Merry Christmas Eve to you, too, Maid Marian," he said. "What are you ladies doing out this evening?"

Marian said, "I've been out delivering baskets to the poor."

"There are so many in need," said Lady Kluck. "We've just run out."

Robin smiled wide. "It just so happens that I was doing the same thing. Let us share these gifts with you."

The sheriff's Christmas trimmings were safely tucked into the carriage. "See you back in Sherwood Forest," Robin called as Little John pulled the sleigh off into the woods. He stayed to hand out the food and gifts with Maid Marian. When they finished, they headed for Sherwood Forest to join Little John and the others.

Robin Hood couldn't help but feel that this had been a perfect Christmas. He'd given plenty of food and good cheer to the people of Nottingham. And he had the best gift of all—spending his holiday with Maid Marian.

The Perfect Gift

Christmas was just a few days away. Geppetto, the old wood-carver, was busy making toy soldiers and pretty dolls for the boys and girls in the village. There seemed to be more toys than usual to make this year. Geppetto was afraid that he wouldn't get all the work done in time.

Geppetto's son, Pinocchio, was eager to help his father. He knew Geppetto worked harder during the Christmas season than at any other time of the year. While Geppetto worked day and night to make all the toys, Pinocchio,  with the help of Jiminy Cricket, decorated the house for the holidays. Then they put up a tree and strung popcorn on its branches. They hung garlands of holly.

This would be Pinocchio's first Christmas as a real boy. He wanted it to be very special.

"Jiminy," Pinocchio said, "I want to find the perfect gift for Geppetto. He should have something special. Will you help me?"

"Hmm," Jiminy said. "Well, if you ask me—"

"Maybe he would like a new knife to carve with?" Pinocchio said. Then he realized he probably didn't have enough money for that. "Oh, what about some warm gloves? He could use them when he goes out on cold nights to deliver toys."

"You know, Pinocchio, I wonder if a better gift would be—" Jiminy began.

"Socks!" Pinocchio cried. "Or a new hat! Come on, Jiminy, let's go to the shops and see what we can find." Pinocchio hurried out the door. Jiminy had to run to keep up.

In the shops, Pinocchio looked at socks, warm hats, gloves, scarves, and even a warm woolen coat. But everything was too small, too expensive, or too ordinary. Pinocchio wanted to find something *special*.

By Christmas Eve, Pinocchio still hadn't found the perfect gift for Geppetto. He felt sad.

"What am I going to do?" he asked Jiminy.

"Well, I do have this idea," the cricket said.

"Really?" Pinocchio asked. "Please tell me!"

Jiminy sat him at the table and handed him a quill pen.

"You want to give your father something he really needs?"

"I sure do." Pinocchio beamed.

"Write this," Jiminy said. "Dear Geppetto, my gift to you is an extra pair of hands and an extra-willing heart. Love, Pinocchio."

When Pinocchio finished writing, he looked up at Jiminy. "Now what?" he asked.

"Now you put the note in here." Jiminy held out a box. Pinocchio dropped the note in. Then Jiminy wrapped the package with bright paper and a big bow.

"Geppetto will be very happy with this gift," Jiminy said.

"But it's just a scrap of paper," Pinocchio said. "What sort of gift is that?"

Jiminy smiled. "You might be surprised."

Geppetto took a break from his work to share Christmas Eve dinner with his son. After the meal, Pinocchio gave Geppetto his gift.

"What's this?" he asked.

"Your Christmas present," Pinocchio replied. "I hope you like it."

Geppetto untied the bow and tore the wrapping paper away. "Why . . . this is the perfect present!" he exclaimed. "I could use an extra pair of hands in my workshop. How did you know, Pinocchio?"

Pinocchio just smiled. Jiminy had been right—he was surprised at how much joy his gift brought to his father.

"I'm glad to help," Pinocchio said. "I can start right now if you want."

Pinocchio cleared the dinner dishes from the table. He washed them and put them away. Then he went to Geppetto's workshop. He swept up the wood shavings and boxed and wrapped the new toys. He made labels for each box so Geppetto would know who each gift was for.

When Geppetto set out to deliver the last of the gifts, Pinocchio went up to bed. He was tired after helping his father all night. But he was also very pleased that he made his father so happy. As he drifted off to sleep, he promised himself that he would help out more often.

That night, the Blue Fairy appeared. "Because you have been so thoughtful this year, I came to grant you one very special Christmas wish," she said. "Think carefully about what you want."

Pinocchio thought about the many things he could ask for. But he still only wanted one thing. "I want to give Geppetto the *perfect* Christmas gift," he told the Blue Fairy. "Something that he will love forever."

The Blue Fairy smiled. She knew just what that present should be. "You are a very kind and loving boy, Pinocchio," she said. "I'm sure Geppetto will treasure this gift for years to come."

The next morning, Geppetto woke up early. He quietly went downstairs to light the fire and make breakfast. He was so happy that Pinocchio had helped him the night before that he wanted to surprise his son. He wanted Pinocchio's first Christmas to be special.

Geppetto went to place his gifts for Pinocchio under the tree. He had carved a beautiful toy rocking horse and had crafted a playful jack-in-the-box. When he looked at the tree, he paused. Then he gasped.

A puppet that looked exactly like his son hung from the branches. "My dear Pinocchio!" Geppetto said with a smile.

He examined the puppet. It looked just like a puppet he had made a long time ago. One lonely night, he had made a wish on the Wishing Star that the puppet would turn into a real boy. The Blue Fairy had granted his wish, and that was when Pinocchio the puppet had become his son.

When Pinocchio heard his father, he and Jiminy ran downstairs. "Merry Christmas!" he shouted.

Geppetto sat in his favorite chair, holding the puppet. "My gift! How did you make it?"

Pinocchio stared at the copy of the puppet he used to be. He smiled. The Blue Fairy had chosen the perfect present for his father.

"Puppet Pinocchio was my favorite creation," Geppetto said. "Oh, how I've missed him."

A frown appeared on Pinocchio's face. "You have?" he asked. "Have I disappointed you?"

Geppetto laughed. "Not at all, son. You've been perfect in every way. This toy reminds me how very much I wanted a real son. He reminds me of how happy I am to have you."

Pinocchio smiled. He went over to the puppet and looked at it closely. He felt as if he was looking in a mirror—the puppet had the same dark hair and blue eyes he did.

Geppetto stood up and started dancing with the puppet and singing. Pinocchio clapped along. He was thrilled that his father was so happy.

Stopping to catch his breath, Geppetto looked at his son and said, "No one has ever thought to give me a toy of my own to play with because I'm a toy maker. But you understand how much I love toys, Pinocchio. Thank you, son."

"See," Jiminy whispered to Pinocchio, "I told you that you would be surprised. And now you've been surprised twice!"

Pinocchio nodded as he watched his father dance with the puppet some more. Then he went over and danced beside the puppet that looked so much like him.

Geppetto held out the strings for Pinocchio so he could try to make the puppet dance himself. It was difficult, because the puppet was the same size as Pinocchio. But he didn't care. He was happy to share this moment with his father.

A little later, Pinocchio opened the gifts Geppetto had placed under the tree for him. He laughed as the jack-in-the-box popped up, and he rocked the small wooden horse across the floor. But the best present he'd gotten had come from the Blue Fairy. He would never forget the smile on his father's face. He hoped they would share many more holidays just like this one.

Disney · PIXAR
WALL·E

A Gift for WALL-E

WALL-E and EVE peeked over the top of a pile of garbage. The humans were acting very strangely. What were they up to now?

They saw two men stringing small colored lights along a rusty iron fence. Another set up a plastic statue of a fat, white-bearded man in a red suit, red hat, and black boots. A woman propped up a fake silver tree and decorated it with shiny red and green glass balls. Now that people had returned to live on Earth along with robots, they were always doing something that surprised WALL-E and EVE. But even for humans they were acting very strangely.

Weirdest of all, the Captain from the Axiom was singing in a loud, joyful voice!

WALL-E and EVE listened to the words carefully. Confused, they looked at each other. Rudolph? A glowing nose? They thought Rudolph must be a kind of robot, like WALL-E and EVE. But neither of them had ever heard of a reindeer-bot before!

WALL-E and EVE sneaked closer to where the humans were working. They called their bot friends over. While all the robots watched curiously, the humans hung a green circle with small red dots on a storefront. More of the humans started singing. One small girl even shook a silver ball.

Some of the robots had seen behavior like this before, when they were living on the spaceship *Axiom*. It seemed to happen every twelve months. They had never been able to figure it out.

WALL-E looked closely at the humans. He tried to figure out what made this so different. Then he put his little metal finger on it. The humans looked happy! Most of the time on the *Axiom* they had looked tired and bored. But there was something about what they were doing right now, here on Earth, that made them very happy.

If it made the humans so happy, WALL-E thought that maybe it would make the robots happy, too!

For hours, the robots studied the humans. They stored what they had seen in their computer brains. Next they set out to copy the humans.

Some of the bots picked up trash that the humans had used: bits of tinsel, fake holly, and scraps of brightly colored paper.

The light bots collected hundreds of strings of lights. WALL-E already had a couple in his trailer. He'd always thought they were pretty, and Eve loved them. The bots draped WALL-E's trailer with lights. When the electricity was turned on, the lights shined so brightly they looked like a supernova.

M-O hung up old socks on the other wall. He had no idea why anyone would want to put socks on the wall. But if the humans were doing it, so would he!

Vacuum-bot sucked up boxes and boxes of packing peanuts. Unfortunately, he also vacuumed up a nose full of dust. "Ahhhh-chOOOO!" he sneezed. Little white peanuts floated down from the air, coating the floor like a blanket of snow.

WALL-E and EVE roamed the grounds outside the trailer looking for more things to use. WALL-E went one way. EVE went the other.

EVE picked up a piece of shiny metal. She found some scraps of wrapping paper. She stored them inside her chest cavity. Suddenly, she heard two humans talking. One of them was the Captain.

"I just love Christmas, don't you?" the other
human said. "The lights, the decorations, the cookies,
the presents. Christmas is my favorite time of year!"

Christmas! What a lovely word! EVE rolled
it around in her mind. It sparked all
her circuits. Was this the name for
what the humans were doing?

She stopped to listen
more closely to what they
were saying.

"Yes," said the Captain slowly.
"But don't forget, Christmas isn't about
things. That's just what Buy-n-Large
wants us to believe. It's about *giving*,
not just *getting* presents. It's about showing
your friends and family that you care."

The Captain's words hummed inside EVE. Robots didn't have family, but they did have friends. And she had one friend who meant more to her than any other—WALL-E. He had come to save her when she was on the ship. He had given her his spare parts. He had cared for her and watched over her. She needed to show him that she appreciated him.

But what kind of a present would do that?

EVE roamed far and wide. She searched and searched. She found many pieces of junk. None of them were quite right. Then, far from WALL-E's trailer, her gaze locked on the perfect present.

Two days later, it was Christmas Eve. The bots had prepared a celebration just like the humans'. Some of the smaller bots were stirring with excitement. The umbrella bot wore a pointy red hat with a white pom-pom on top.

The robots beeped out the words to the songs they had heard. They didn't always understand the human words so they made up some of their own.

While all the bots were celebrating the holiday in their own high-tech way, EVE pulled WALL-E aside. She held out a present wrapped in pretty patterned paper.

WALL-E looked surprised. "Ee-vah?" he asked.

EVE nodded.

WALL-E turned the present this way and that. He admired how the shiny paper shimmered in the colored lights. He was so busy looking at the present that he almost missed EVE motioning to him.

Open it, EVE signaled.

WALL-E carefully unwrapped the present. He folded up each scrap of paper and laid it on the ground next to him. Finally, he pulled away the last piece.

WALL-E held a little evergreen tree in his hands, a miniature Christmas tree.

The longer version of EVE's name was Extra-terrestrial Vegetation Evaluator. She had been trained to find plants and was drawn to this little tree. She knew that WALL-E, with his kind ways and big heart, would take care of this present, this living thing, better than anyone.

WALL-E and EVE went outside. Together they dug a hole in the earth and planted the Christmas tree. WALL-E placed a shiny silver star on the top.

WALL-E and EVE looked at the tree. The star twinkled brightly. It reflected the light from the real stars shining in the night sky, far above.

EVE reached out her hand. WALL-E took it. "Ee-vah," he said.

Now he understood why humans liked Christmas so much.

The Puppies'
Messy Christmas

One winter evening, Pongo and Perdita were watching TV with their puppies when a rustling noise in the hallway caught their attention. The puppies jumped off their chairs and ran to the doorway.

They all watched silently as Roger and Nanny hauled a huge tree into the parlor. It was fresh and green and made the room smell like a pine forest.

"What's going on?" Rolly asked, turning to look at his mother.

"Don't worry, dear," said Perdita. "It's Christmas Eve. This is just the beginning!"

"Chris-mess?" Lucky asked. "It *does* look like a mess." He wagged his tail.

The parlor floor was covered with pine needles, boxes of ornaments, tinsel garlands, and strings of small lights.

Anita was waiting in the parlor to help Roger and Nanny. The puppies looked on in awe as their human pets began acting very strangely. Roger hung shiny colored globes on the branches. Anita was winding a garland around the tree.

When the tree was finished and the room tidied, Roger flipped a switch. The lights and shiny ornaments cast a magical glow about the room. The puppies looked wide-eyed at the tree.

That night, when Pongo and Perdita tucked the puppies into their basket, they told them all about Christmas.

"It's a time when people show their families and friends how much they care for them," Pongo said. He explained how humans sent cards, baked cookies and fruitcakes, and sang festive carols.

"It may sound strange, but you'll grow to love the holiday season," Perdita said. She nuzzled Patch, who let out a yawn.

"Especially the beef bones left over from dinner," Pongo added.

"Bones?" Patch said, perking up. His father smiled.

"And that's not all," Perdita continued. "On Christmas Eve, after everyone's in bed, people sneak presents under the tree."

"Presents?" all the puppies said at once.

"What kind of presents?" Patch asked. "Can you wish for them?"

"I'd wish for a new bed," Lucky said as he climbed into the basket he shared with his brothers and sisters.

"Why do people put presents under the tree?" Pepper asked.

"Christmas is about giving," Pongo told the puppies. "People give presents to their friends and family to show how much they love them."

"I wonder if we will get any presents?" said Rolly.

"Maybe," Perdita replied. "Anita gave me a new collar last year."

"And I got a red ball," said Pongo.

"I hope someone loves us," said Penny.

"You are all loved, whether or not there are presents under the tree," Perdita said. "Now time for bed. Tomorrow is a big day."

On Christmas morning, the puppies woke at dawn. They crept into the parlor. Sure enough, there were piles of brightly wrapped packages under the tree.

"We *are* loved!" Freckles cried.

The puppies dove into the pile of presents. They tossed the packages around and ripped and tore at the colored paper.

"Christmas is fun!" Rolly exclaimed as he shook some wrapping paper out of his mouth.

291

Lucky pulled open a box. "Perfume?" he said, and wrinkled his nose.

Penny dragged a spotted necktie out of some tissue paper. "What do I need with more spots?"

Freckles held up a lace handkerchief. "What is this for?" he asked.

Just then, they heard Roger's and Anita's voices in the hallway.

The puppies looked at each other in alarm.

"Let's get out of here!" Rolly said. The puppies scampered around the room, hiding behind the sofa, under the chairs, and in the folds of the curtains.

The puppies trembled when they heard Roger's footsteps. He stopped in the doorway. "What on earth?" he said.

Anita walked up beside him. "Oh, dear!" she cried.

"Perdita, Pongo," Roger called out. "Where are you?"

The puppies heard the click of their parents' claws on the wooden floor as they scurried toward the parlor.

When they came into the room, Pongo said, "Woof!"

And Perdita repeated, "Woof!"

The puppies looked at each other uncertainly. "We're in for it now," Lucky whispered.

Then they heard something very strange. Anita started to laugh.

Roger said, with a chuckle, "Looks like we had some help opening our gifts."

"Wasn't that kind of the puppies!" Nanny said as she walked into the room and saw the mess of paper and ribbon.

"I wonder where they've gone off to," Roger said with a twinkle in his eye. "Here, pups!"

"There are still so many boxes to unwrap," Anita said, shaking her head. "I do wish they'd come and help."

The puppies slowly crept out from their hiding places and gathered around the tree.

Roger pointed to the packages. "Go for it, boys and girls!"

Yip! Yip! The puppies attacked the presents, tearing into the bright wrappings and the tangled ribbons.

When the puppies grew tired of rolling around in the wrapping paper, Anita brought out a large basket.

"Sorry we didn't have time to wrap these," she said. "But then . . ." She smiled. ". . . maybe you've done enough work for today."

She handed each puppy a squeaky toy.

From the bottom of the basket she pulled out two Christmas sweaters for Pongo and Perdita.

"Anita knitted them herself," said Roger with pride.

That evening, after Christmas dinner was over, the puppies were still full of energy. They weren't ready to go to bed.

"We like Christmas!" said Pepper.

"We like our toys!" said Rolly.

"We like wrapping paper!" said Patch.

"But remember what we told you about Christmas?" Perdita asked. She nudged her children toward their basket. "It's a time for giving."

"It's also about *forgiving*," Pongo said gently. "You were lucky that Roger and Anita weren't upset that you unwrapped their presents."

The puppies' heads drooped a little.

"We're lucky we have two wonderful humans," Perdita said softly. "That is the best present of all." The puppies raised their eyes to their mother hopefully.

"We are loved," Penny said. She smiled.

"You are all, each and every one of you, loved," Perdita assured her children.

"And that's what Christmas is really all about," Pongo said as the puppies drifted off to sleep.